John Ford's The Lady's Trial: A Retelling

David Bruce

Published by David Bruce, 2022.

JOHN FORD'S THE LADY'S TRIAL: A RETELLING

First edition. July 9, 2022.

Copyright © 2022 David Bruce.

ISBN: 979-8201579395

Written by David Bruce.

Table of Contents

CAST OF CHARACTERS..1
PROLOGUE..3
CHAPTER 1 | — 1.1 —..5
— 1.2 —...16
— 1.3 —...23
CHAPTER 2 | — 2.1 —...27
— 2.2 —...37
— 2.3 —...42
— 2.4 —...43
CHAPTER 3 | — 3.1 —...48
— 3.2 —...57
— 3.3 —...60
— 3.4 —...68
CHAPTER 4 | — 4.1 —...72
— 4.2 —...77
— 4.3 —...87
CHAPTER 5 | — 5.1 —...98
— 5.2 —...103
EPILOGUE..119
APPENDIX A: NOTES | — 1.1 —...120
— 4.3 —...126
— 4.3 —...127
— 5.2 —...128
— Entire Play —..129
APPENDIX B: ABOUT THE AUTHOR.................................130
APPENDIX C: SOME BOOKS BY DAVID BRUCE........................131

Dedication

Dedicated to Carl Eugene Bruce and Josephine Saturday Bruce

My father, Carl Eugene Bruce, died on 24 October 2013. He used to work for Ohio Power, and at one time, his job was to shut off the electricity of people who had not paid their bills. He sometimes would find a home with an impoverished mother and some children. Instead of shutting off their electricity, he would tell the mother that she needed to pay her bill or soon her electricity would be shut off. He would write on a form that no one was home when he stopped by because if no one was home he did not have to shut off their electricity.

The best good deed that anyone ever did for my father occurred after a storm that knocked down many power lines. He and other linemen worked long hours and got wet and cold. Their feet were freezing because water got into their boots and soaked their socks. Fortunately, a kind woman gave my father and the other linemen dry socks to wear.

My mother, Josephine Saturday Bruce, died on 14 June 2003. She used to work at a store that sold clothing. One day, an impoverished mother with a baby clothed in rags walked into the store and started shoplifting in an interesting way: The mother took the rags off her baby and dressed the infant in new clothing. My mother knew that this mother could not afford to buy the clothing, but she helped the mother dress her baby and then she watched as the mother walked out of the store without paying.

***

The doing of good deeds is important. As a free person, you can choose to live your life as a good person or as a bad person. To be a good person, do good deeds. To be a bad person, do bad deeds. If you do good deeds, you will become good. If you do bad deeds, you will become bad. To become the person you want to be, act as if you already are that kind of person. Each of us chooses what kind of person we will become. To become a good person, do the things a good person does. To become a bad person, do the things a bad person does. The opportunity to take action to become the kind of person you want to be is yours.

Human beings have free will. According to the Babylonian Niddah 16b, whenever a baby is to be conceived, the Lailah (angel in charge of contraception) takes the drop of semen that will result in the conception and asks God, "Sovereign of the Universe, what is going to be the fate of this drop? Will it develop into a robust or into a weak person? An intelligent or a stupid person? A wealthy or a poor person?" The Lailah asks all these questions, but it does not ask, "Will it develop into a righteous or a wicked person?" The answer to that question lies in the decisions to be freely made by the human being that is the result of the conception.

A Buddhist monk visiting a class wrote this on the chalkboard: "EVERYONE WANTS TO SAVE THE WORLD, BUT NO ONE WANTS TO HELP MOM DO THE DISHES." The students laughed, but the monk then said, "Statistically, it's highly unlikely that any of you will ever have the opportunity to run into a burning orphanage and rescue an infant. But, in the smallest gesture of kindness — a warm smile, holding the door for the person behind you, shoveling the driveway of the elderly person next door — you have committed an act of immeasurable profundity, because to each of us, our life is our universe."

In her book titled *I Have Chosen to Stay and Fight*, comedian Margaret Cho writes, "I believe that we get complimentary snack-size portions of the afterlife, and we all receive them in a different way." For Ms. Cho, many of her snack-size portions of the afterlife come in hip hop music. Other people get different snack-size portions of the afterlife, and we all must be on the lookout for them when they come our way. And perhaps doing good deeds and experiencing good deeds are snack-size portions of the afterlife.

The Zen master Gisan was taking a bath. The water was too hot, so he asked a student to add some cold water to the bath. The student brought a bucket of cold water, added some cold water to the bath, and then threw the rest of the water on a rocky path. Gisan scolded the student: "Everything can be used. Why did you waste the rest of the water by pouring it on the path? There are some plants nearby which could have used the water. What right do you have to waste even a drop of water?" The student became enlightened and changed his name to Tekisui, which means "Drop of Water."

Cover Photo for John Ford's *The Lady's Trial*: A Retelling:
https://pixabay.com/photos/portrait-krupnyj-plan-skin-person-
4400419/

***

According to Charles Lamb, "Ford was of the first order of poets. He sought for sublimity, not by parcels in metaphors or visible images, but directly where she has her full residence in the heart of man; in the actions and sufferings of the greatest minds."

Educate Yourself
Read Like A Wolf Eats
Be Excellent to Each Other
Books Then, Books Now, Books Forever

***

In this retelling, as in all my retellings, I have tried to make the work of literature accessible to modern readers who may lack the knowledge about mythology, religion, and history that the literary work's contemporary audience had.

Do you know a language other than English? If you do, I give you permission to translate this book, copyright your translation, publish or self-publish it, and keep all the royalties for yourself. (Do give me credit, of course, for the original retelling.)

I would like to see my retellings of classic literature used in schools, so I give permission to the country of Finland (and all other countries) to give copies of this book to all students forever. I also give permission to the state of Texas (and all other states) to give copies of this book to all students forever. I also give permission to all teachers to give copies of this book to all students forever.

Teachers need not actually teach my retellings. Teachers are welcome to give students copies of my eBooks as background material. For example, if they are teaching Homer's *Iliad* and *Odyssey*, teachers are welcome to give students copies of my *Virgil's* Aeneid: *A Retelling in Prose* and tell students, "Here's another ancient epic you may want to read in your spare time."

CAST OF CHARACTERS

Male Characters

Auria, a nobleman of Genoa, married to Spinella.

Lord Adurni, a young lord.

Aurelio, friend to Auria.

Malfato, a discontented lover, cousin of Spinella and Castanna. The Latin *fatum malum* means "bad fate."

Trelcatio, a citizen of Genoa, uncle of Auria, and father of Amoretta. He is an old man.

Martino, a citizen of Genoa and great-uncle of Levidolce.

Piero, a dependent on Lord Adurni.

Futelli, a dependent on Lord Adurni.

Guzman the Spaniard, a braggadocio Spaniard and out-of-work soldier. His command of English is not perfect, so he probably speaks with a not-exaggerated Spanish accent.

Fulgoso the Parvenu, an upstart gallant. His catchphrase is "as it were." He is a parvenu: He has enjoyed a recent large rise in wealth and social status. His family made money by selling provisions to Dutch soldiers, so he probably speaks with a slight Dutch accent. He whistles.

Benazzi, divorced husband to Levidolce.

Female Characters

Spinella, wife to Auria. A spinel is a precious stone.

Castanna, her sister. The Latin *casta* means "chaste."

Amoretta, a fantastic maiden. A fantastic person is a fanciful person. She lisps and is obsessed with princes and the number of horses that pull their carriages. Trelcatio is her father, and Auria is her cousin. Amoretta's lisp turns S's into Th's, and G's into D's, and sometimes R's into W's or other sounds.

Levidolce, a wanton. Her name contains Italian words meaning "light" and "sweet." A wanton woman is a lustful woman who pursues unchaste sex.

Scene

Genoa, Italy.

Notes:

In this culture, a man of higher rank would use words such as "thee," "thy," "thine," and "thou" to refer to a servant. However, two close friends or a husband and wife could properly use "thee," "thy," "thine," and "thou" to refer to each other.

The word "sirrah" is a term usually used to address a man of lower social rank than the speaker. This was socially acceptable, but sometimes the speaker would use the word as an insult when speaking to a man whom he did not usually call "sirrah." Close friends, whether male or female, could also call each other "sirrah."

A main theme of this play is the use of ambiguous language to avoid stating what could be unpleasant truths. Characters in this play tend not to be after the truth, the whole truth, and nothing the truth. Instead, they use ambiguous language to bring about a happy ending.

PROLOGUE

"Language and matter, with a fit of mirth

"That sharply savors more of air than earth,

"Like midwives, bring a play to timely birth."

Note: John Ford identifies three characteristics of a good play: Language, matter (content), and mirth that is more spiritual than earthly — that is, more spiritual than bawdy.

"But where's now such a one in which these three

"Are handsomely contrived? Or, if they be,

"Are understood by all who hear to see?"

Note: John Ford criticizes both playwrights and audiences. Where is a good play nowadays? And if there are good plays, where are the intelligent audiences who can appreciate them? Audiences both hear and see a play.

"Wit, wit's the word in fashion, that alone

"Cries up [proclaims] the poet, which, though neatly [elegantly] shown.

"Is rather censured, oftentimes, than known."

Note: John Ford identifies a fourth characteristic of good plays: wit, aka intelligence. Unfortunately, true wit is often criticized rather than recognized.

"He who will venture on a jest, that can

"Rail on another's pain, or idly scan

"Affairs of state, oh, he's the only man!"

Note: John Ford notes that critics and audiences often appreciate only references to current affairs and the personalities involved in them.

"A goodly approbation, which must bring

"Fame with contempt by such a deadly sting!

"The Muses chatter, who were wont to sing."

Note: John Ford criticizes such reliance on current events and personalities. Approval of such plays should be treated with contempt because such plays make the Muses chatter rather than sing.

"Your favors in what we present today;

"Our fearless author boldly bids me say

"He tenders you no satire, but a play;"

Note: John Ford asks the audience to favor his play, which is a real play —
one that seeks to make the Muses sing.

"In which, if so he have not hit all right.

"For wit, words, mirth, and matter as he might.

"He wishes yet he had, for your delight."

Note: John Ford recognizes that he may not have written the excellent play
he wanted to write, but if he has not, he wishes he had because an excellent play
would delight the audience, including you, the readers of this book.

CHAPTER 1

— 1.1 —

Piero and Futelli, both of whom worked for a young lord named Lord Adurni, entered a room in Auria's house from different doors and met.

Piero said, "Accomplished man of fashion!"

Futelli said, "The times' wonder! Gallant of gallants, Genoa's Piero!"

They were members of a mutual admiration society.

Piero said, "Italy's darling, Europe's joy, and so forth! What is the newest news? The newest and unvarnished news?"

"I am no foot-messenger," Futelli replied. "I am no peddler of official dispatches, no monopolist of newsletters of dubious credibility, no monger of gazettes."

Piero said, "You are a monger of courtesans, my fine Futelli. In a certain way you are a merchant of the staple for wares of use and trade — a taker-up. Rather indeed a knocker-down; the word will carry either sense."

Piero was calling Futelli a whoremonger. He was a taker-up of skirts, and he used whores to knock down his erections.

Piero continued, "But, in pure earnest, how trolls the common noise? How wag the tongues of the people around us?"

Futelli replied, "Auria, who was lately wedded and bedded to the fair Spinella, tired with the enjoyments of delights, is hastening to cuff the Turkish pirates in the service of the Great Duke of Florence."

At this time, some citizens of Italian cities and some citizens of Turkey were fighting.

Piero asked, "Won't he carry his pretty thing along with him when he goes to the wars?"

His pretty thing was his new wife: Spinella.

One meaning of the word "thing" is genitals, whether male or female.

Futelli replied, "He leaves her to buffet land-pirates here at home."

By leaving his wife at home without him to protect her, Auria was giving an opportunity to men — Italian land-pirates — to attempt to seduce her.

"Italian land-pirates?" Piero said. "Sirrah, that's thou and I: you, Futelli, and I, Piero."

He then said about Auria, "Blockhead! To run from such an armful of pleasures in order to gain — what? — a bloody nose of honor. This action is most sottish — stupid — and abominable!"

"It is wicked, shameful, and cowardly, I will maintain," Futelli said.

Piero asked, "Is all my signor's hospitality — huge banquets, deep revels, and costly trappings — shrunk to a cabin, and a single welcome to beverage and biscuit?"

To fight against Turkish pirates, Auria would have to sail. He would be cooped up in a ship's cabin, and he would be eating sea biscuits.

Futelli said, "Hold thy peace, man. It makes for us — he comes; let's part and look grave and serious."

Futelli was going to say that Auria's absence would give them the opportunity to attempt to seduce Spinella, Auria's wife, but Auria's arrival forced him to stop speaking.

Futelli and Piero assumed serious expressions and stood in different parts of the room.

Auria and Lord Adurni, his friend, walked into the room.

Lord Adurni said, "We wish thee, honored Auria, life and safety. Return crowned with a victory whose wreath of triumph may advance thy country's glory, worthy your name and ancestors!"

"My lord," Auria said, "I shall not live to thrive in any action deserving memory, when I forget Lord Adurni's love and favor."

Piero stepped forward and said, "I present to you my service for a farewell; let few words excuse all arts of compliment."

Futelli stepped forward and said, "As for my own part, kill or be killed — for there's the short and long of it — call me your shadow's hench-boy."

A hench-boy is a page of honor, an attendant of honor.

Auria said to Lord Adurni, Piero, and Futelli, "Gentlemen, my business, which requires immediate haste, forces me to reply briefly."

Lord Adurni replied, "We dare not hinder your resolution winged with thoughts so constant. We wish all happiness to you!"

Piero and Futelli said, "We wish all satisfactions to you!"

Lord Adurni, Piero, and Futelli exited.

Auria said to himself, "Just as the wintered people living in the north leave the minutes of their summer, when the sun departs and leaves them in cold robes of ice, so I leave Genoa."

Trelcatio, Spinella, and Castanna walked into the room. Trelcatio was Auria's uncle, Spinella was Auria's newly wedded wife, and Castanna was Auria's sister-in-law.

Seeing them coming toward him, Auria said to himself, "Now appears the object of my apprenticed heart."

He then said out loud, "Thou bring, Spinella, a welcome in a farewell — souls and bodies are severed for a time, a span of time. But on the Day of Judgment, they join again, without all separation, in a confirmed unity forever.

"Such will our next embraces be, for the rest of our lives; and then taking heed of our divisions and enjoying the rest of our lives together will sweeten the remembrance of past dangers, will fasten love in perpetuity and will force our sleeps to steal upon our stories. These days must come, and shall, without a cloud or night of fear or envy."

Auria and his wife, Spinella, would be separated while he was fighting the Turkish pirates, but he would then return and they would be happy together for the rest of their lives. Because they would be so happy together, their sleeps — deaths — would be forced to steal upon them.

Auria then said to his uncle, "To your charge, Trelcatio, our good uncle, and to the comfort of my Spinella's sister, fair Castanna, I entrust this treasure."

Trelcatio replied, "I dare to promise to husband that trust with truth and care."

Castanna said, "My sister shall to me stand as an example of pouring free devotions for your safety."

Ancient people used to pour offerings of wine and milk to the gods as they prayed.

Auria replied, "Gentle Castanna, thou are a branch of goodness grown on the self-same stock with my Spinella."

The sisters Spinella and Castanna came from the same family tree.

To Spinella, who had remained silent, he said, "But why, my dear, have thou locked up thy speech in so much silent sadness? Oh, at parting, it seems that one private whisper must be sighed."

He then said to Trelcatio, "Uncle, may the best of peace enrich your family! I take my leave."

This was a hint for him to leave so that Auria could talk privately with Spinella and her sister.

Trelcatio replied, "May blessings and health preserve you!"

He exited.

Castanna began to exit, but Auria said, "Nay, nay, Castanna, you may hear what Spinella and I say to each other. For a while you are designated to be your sister's husband."

By "husband," he meant companion and protector.

He then said, "Give me thy hand, Spinella. You promised to send me away from you with more cheerful looks, without a grudge or tear; indeed, love, you promised that."

Spinella asked, "What friend do I have left in your absence?"

"You have many friends," Auria answered. "Thy virtues are such friends that they cannot fail thee. They are faith, purity of thoughts, and such a meekness as would force scandal to blush."

Spinella said, "Suppose, sir, that the patent of your life should be called in, and you were to die. How am I left then to come to terms with my griefs? I would then be more to be pitied than if I had only a broken heart!

"Auria, soul of my comforts! I let fall no eye on breach of — attack on — fortune. I contemn — scorn — no entertainment to divided hopes. I urge no pressures by the scorn of change."

If her husband were to die, she would be financially hurt. She would not have him to take care of her. She recognized this, but it was something else that hurt her most.

"And yet, my Auria, when I but conceive how easy it is without impossibility never to see thee more, forgive me then, if I conclude I may be miserable, most miserable."

What made Spinella hurt most was the possibility that her husband would die in the fighting and she would never see him again.

Castanna said, "And such a conclusion, sister, argues the effects of a distrust more voluntary than cause by likelihood."

She meant that Spinella's fear was caused more by her emotions than by the likelihood of her husband's death.

One can argue with that. Soldiers and sailors die in war.

Auria said, "You speak the truth, Castanna."

Spinella said, "I grant that it is the truth; yet, Auria, I'm a woman, and therefore I am apt to fear.

"To show my duty, and not take heart — courage — from you, I'll walk away from you, at your command, and not so much as trouble your thought with one poor looking-back."

In this society, her duty was to be an obedient wife. Her husband wanted her to not worry, and so she would refrain from showing her fear as he departed for the war.

Auria said, "I thank thee, my worthy wife! Before we kiss, receive this caution from thine Auria.

"But first, Castanna, let us bid farewell."

Castanna walked aside to give Auria and Spinella some privacy.

Spinella said, "Speak, good Auria, speak."

Auria then began to give his wife his caution: "The steps young ladies tread, left to their own discretion, however wisely printed, are observed, and they are construed as the lookers-on presume."

In other words: Young ladies, when their male protectors are absent, are watched by other people, and the young ladies' actions are interpreted by those observers.

But note: Auria talked about ladies' "printed" steps. Words, whether spoken or printed, are hard to interpret correctly. Printed words, however, have the advantage of opportunities of being revised before being printed.

Auria continued, "Point out thy ways, then, in such even paths that thine own jealousies from others' tongues may not intrude a guilt, though undeserved."

In other words: Behave in such a way that other people cannot misinterpret your actions as guilty.

But note: "Point out" can mean "point out verbally," as well as "direct — manage — your behavior."

And note: "Jealousy" can be "a strong feeling *for* someone, such as devotion" or "a strong feeling *against* someone, such as anger."

And note: To "point" also means to add punctuation to writing to make it clearer.

Auria continued, "Allow visits as of medicine forced, not to procure health, but for safe prevention against a growing sickness."

In other words: Any visits you make or any decisions about which visitors you receive should be undertaken with precaution and prudence. Such respectable visits and visitors will not cause gossip, and since they are so respectable they will prevent gossip.

But note: "Forced" carries the meaning of "subjected to violence," and the verb "force" includes the meaning "rape." If Spinella were to be subjected to a forced visit, even if it were from a respectable man, it would cause gossip, hate, and discontent.

Auria continued, "In thy use of time and of discourse, be found so thrifty as no remembrance may impeach thy rest."

In other words: Your use of time and your conversation should be such as to cause no night thoughts of regret that will later prevent you from sleeping easily.

But note: The word "thrifty" can mean "respectable" and "frugal." Because words are often so difficult to use to convey meaning, it can be best to use them frugally lest they be misinterpreted. Words that you intend to be respectable can be misinterpreted as being scandalous.

Auria continued, "Appear not in a fashion that can prompt the gazer's eye, or cry 'holla,' to report some widowed neglect of handsome value."

In other words: Appear in such a way that gossipers cannot report that you are neglecting good behavior because of lack of your husband's supervision.

But note: The word "fashion" can refer to clothing style or to workmanship or to usage. Words can be fashioned.

And note: "Cry" can refer to a shout or exclamation. A "descry" can mean "the fact of being discovered, usually visually," according to the *Oxford English Dictionary*. The cry of "Holla!" can mean "Stop!"

And note: "Widowed" can mean "deprived of a mate" or "desolate and solitary." "Neglect" can mean "failure to take care of a dependent person," according to the *Oxford English Dictionary*. In this case, "widowed neglect" can refer to Auria's going away and leaving Spinella in Genoa (and so Auria ought to take his own advice).

And note: "Handsome" can be used ironically of a punishment: A "handsome" beating is a "fine" beating.

Auria continued, "In recreations be both wise and free. Live always at home, home to thyself, however enriched with noble company."

In other words: Stay true to your noble and honorable self even when in the midst of noble company. "Free" means noble and honorable, in addition to other meanings.

But note: "Recreations" can mean entertainment, while "re-creations can mean" "new creations." One can re-create oneself, or one can be re-created through gossip.

And note: "Free" can mean "Noble, honorable, not impeded or restrained, allowed to go where one wishes, released from ties of marriage and love" (*Oxford English Dictionary*).

And note: "Wise" can mean "having sound judgment" or "having occult knowledge, like a witch" (*Oxford English Dictionary*).

And note: "Noble" can refer to birth or to character. A person of noble birth need not necessarily have a noble character.

And note: The word "company" can mean "sexual intercourse." If a person is enriched, they acquire something: In sexual intercourse, a little something passes from one person to another.

Auria continued, "Remember that a woman's virtue, in her lifetime, writes the epitaph that all covet on their tombs."

In other words: People covet a good — and deserved — epitaph on their tombs. Such an epitaph can be earned with one's behavior while alive.

But note: We can ask if all women want a virtuous epitaph on their tombs. Women can have a lot of sex with a lot of partners and be proud of it.

And note: The word "covet" is used in sentences such as "Thou shalt not covet thy neighbor's wife."

Auria continued, "In short, I know thou never will forget whose wife thou are, nor how upon thy lips thy husband at his parting sealed this kiss. No more."

He kissed her.

Spinella said, "Dear heaven!"

She then said, "Go, sister, go."

Spinella and Castanna exited.

Auria said about his wife's exit, "Done bravely, and like the choice of glory. To know my own glory, I have forgone one of Earth's best people."

He was leaving his wife to seek glory in war.

Seeing his friend Aurelio enter, Auria said, "See! See! In yet another person I am rich: a friend, a perfect one, Aurelio."

Aurelio said, "Had I been no stranger to your bosom, sir, before now you might have included me in your resolutions, making me the companion of your fortunes."

Auria said, "So the wrongs I should have ventured on against thy fate must have denied all pardon. If I had done that, I would have unpardonably included you in the dangers I will face.

"Let's not have a dispute about why before this present instant I concealed the stealth of my adventures from thy counsels, not telling you about my plans. Therefore, know that my needs drive me away from here."

Aurelio said, "'Needs!' So you said, and it was not spoken like a friend."

A friend would have told Aurelio earlier about what the friend needed but lacked.

"Hear me further," Auria said.

Aurelio said, "Auria, beware of covering up a folly willing to range away from Genoa: Don't be without an excuse discovered in the coinage of untruths."

In other words, Aurelio was saying this: Don't lie to me. Let me know why you are willing to do the foolish action of going away from Genoa — and your wife. Do have an excuse — a reason or apology — for the coinage of lies.

He continued, "I use no harder language. Thou are almost already on a shipwreck, in forsaking the holy land of friendship by forsaking to talk to me about your needs. Damn!"

Auria said, "By that sacred thing last issued from the temple where it dwelt — I mean our friendship — I am sunk so low in my financial estate, that, if you tell me to live in Genoa only six months longer, I will outlast the remnant of all that is left of my wealth."

Aurelio grunted.

Auria said, "In my country, friend — where I have stood beside my superior, friend, swayed the opposition, friend; friend, here to fall subject to scorn, or to rarely found compassion, would be more than a man who has a soul could bear — that is, a man who has a soul not stooped to servitude."

Auria was proud. He did not want to become impoverished in Genoa, where people would scorn him, or, more rarely, feel pity for him.

Aurelio said, "You show neither certainty nor even weak assurance yet, of restoring your wealth in this course of action in case you are offered the responsibility of military command."

Auria said, "He who cannot merit promotions by his employments, let him bare his throat to the Turkish cruelty, or die, or live a slave without redemption!"

He was confident of performing well enough to be promoted, and he was confident that if he were promoted he could restore his wealth.

Aurelio said, "Concerning that, I see! But you have a wife, a young wife, a fair wife; she, although she could never claim right in prosperity, was never tempted by trial of extremes, to youth and beauty baits for dishonor and a perished reputation."

Auria could leave and restore his wealth, but what about his young, beautiful wife? She had never lived in a really wealthy household, and extreme wealth could be a temptation for her to commit sin and lose her good reputation. In other words, it is possible that she could be seduced by a wealthy man while Auria was away from her.

Auria said, "Show me the man who lives, and to my face dares to speak, scarcely to think, such tyranny against Spinella's constancy, except Aurelio — he is my friend."

Auria did not appreciate the suggestion that his wife could be tempted to commit adultery, but Aurelio was and remained his friend.

Aurelio said, "There doesn't live, then, a friend who dares to love you like Aurelio; that Aurelio, who, late and early, said often and truly that your marriage with Spinella would entangle as much the opinion due to your discretion as your estate: It has done so to both."

According to Aurelio, a true friend, such as himself, would bring up inconvenient truths — such as the inconvenient truth that Auria's marrying Spinella, a woman from a family that could not provide a good dowry for her, had harmed both Auria's reputation as a sensible man and his financial estate.

If Auria had married a rich woman, her dowry would have improved both Auria's reputation as a sensible man and his financial estate. Not marrying for money had harmed both his reputation and his financial estate.

Auria agreed with Aurelio: "I find it has."

Aurelio said, "He who prescribes no law, no limits of condition to the objects of his affection, but will merely wed a face because it is round, or painted by nature in purest red and white, which are the colors of beauty, or, at the best, wed a woman because his loved one owns an excellence of qualities, knows when and how to speak, where to keep silence, with fit reasons why, whose virtues are her only dowry, or will wed a woman who has neither beauty nor good qualities to be her only dowry, ought of himself to master such fortunes as add fuel to their loves."

Such fortunes would include financial fortunes. If a man wed such a woman as one of those Aurelio mentioned — and Spinella had both beauty and good qualities — then not worrying about finances would make their love increase.

Aurelio continued, "For otherwise — but herein I am idle, and I have spoken foolishly to little purpose."

"She's my wife," Auria said.

Aurelio replied, "And since she is your wife, it is not manly done to leave her to the trial of her wits, her modesty, her innocence, and her vows. Doing that is a way to point out to her an art of wanton life."

Auria asked, "Sir, did you really mean what you just said?"

Aurelio replied, "You form reasons, just ones, for your abandoning the storms that threaten your own ruin; but you propose no shelter for your wife's honor. What my tongue has uttered, Auria, is just honest fear, and you are wise enough to interpret correctly what I am saying and why I said it."

Auria said, "Necessity must arm my confidence, which if I live to triumph over my need, friend, and if I ever come back with plenty of wealth, I pronounce Aurelio the heir of what I can bequeath, with some fit deduction — a suitable sum of money set aside — for a worthy widow allowed, with the assumption that she is likely to prove to be so worthy."

If he returned with wealth after fighting the Turkish pirates, he would make Aurelio his heir of what was left of his wealth after giving his widow a share to provide for her, provided she was worthy of receiving it.

"Who?" Aurelio said. "You make me your heir? Your wife is yet so young, and she is in every probability so likely to make you a father! Set aside such thoughts as making me your heir."

Auria said, "Believe it without making replies and objections, Aurelio. Keep this note: It is a warrant for receiving from Martino two hundred ducats. As you find it suitable, give them in my absence to Spinella. I would not trust her uncle; he, good man, is at an ebb in finances himself. Another hundred ducats I left with her; yet another hundred ducats I carry with me.

"Am I not poor, Aurelio, now? The exchange of more debates between us would undo my resolution.

"Walk a little with me, please. Friends we are, and we will embrace as friends, but let's not speak another word."

"I'll follow you to your horse," Aurelio said.

They exited.

In a room in Lord Adurni's house, Futelli gave a letter to Lord Adurni. Futelli was a dependent of Lord Adurni, a young lord whom Futelli served. The letter was written by a recently divorced woman named Levidolce, whose name contains Italian words meaning "light" and "sweet."

Lord Adurni asked, "She wrote this with her own hand?"

In Levidolce's society, many young women were not educated.

Futelli replied, "She never used, my lord, a second means — an agent to write the letter for her — but kissed the letter first, looked over the superscription naming the recipient of the letter; then let fall some amorous tears of love, kissed it again, talked to it twenty times over, set it to her mouth, gave it to me, snatched it back again, and then cried, 'Oh, my poor heart!' and, in an instant, 'Commend my truth and secrecy.'

"Such medley of passion I never saw yet in woman."

"In woman?" Lord Adurni said. "Thou are deceived. Except that we both had mothers, I could say how women are, in their own natures, models of mere change — of change of what is bad to what is worse."

He hesitated and then asked, "She tipped you liberally?"

"She forced on me twenty ducats," Futelli said, "and she vowed, by the precious love she bore the 'best of men' — I use, my lord, her exact words — 'the miracle of men, Malfato' — then she sighed — this 'mite of gold' was 'only entrance to a farther bounty.' It is meant, my lord, likely to be press-money."

When a man was drafted into the army or navy — that is, pressed into military service — he was given a sum of money. Futelli believed that the tip that Levidolce had given to him was press-money: He would be delivering many more love letters and running other amatory errands for her.

Lord Adurni said, "Devil! How dared she to tempt thee, Futelli, knowing thy love to me?"

Levidolce should have known that Futelli was loyal to Lord Adurni.

Futelli replied, "There lies, my lord, her cunning, or rather her craftiness. First she began by saying what a pity it was that men should differ in financial estates without proportion: Some men are so strangely rich, while other men are so miserably poor. 'And yet,' said she, 'since it is truly indeed unfit that all men should be equals, so I must confess that it is good justice that the most proper men should be preferred to fortune — the men such as nature had marked with fair abilities; of which men Genoa, for anything I know, has wondrously few — not two to boast of.'"

"Here began her sexual itch," Lord Adurni said.

Futelli said, "I answered that a woman would be happy, then, whose choice in you, my lord, was singular."

If Lord Adurni were her singular choice, he would be the only man she slept with. Of course, a singular choice can be a superior choice.

"Well urged," Lord Adurni said, smiling.

Futelli said, "She smiled, and said it might be so, and yet — there she stopped. So then I concluded with her that the title of a lord was not enough for absolute perfection; I had seen persons of meaner quality much more exact in fair endowments — but your lordship will pardon me, I hope."

"Yes, and love thee for it," Lord Adurni said.

"Phew!" Futelli said. As one of Lord Adurni's dependents, he wanted to stay on his good side and not say anything that would insult him.

He continued, "'Let that pass,' said she; 'and now that we prattle of handsome gentlemen, in my opinion Malfato is a very pretty fellow. Isn't he, I ask you, sir?'

"I had then the truth of what I aimed to find out, and with more than praise, I approved her judgment in so high a strain of expression, saying that he was without comparison, my honored lord, that soon we both reached a decision about the man, the match, and the business."

Lord Adurni asked, "You reached the decision to deliver a letter to Malfato?"

"Yes," Futelli said. "Whereto I no sooner had consented, with protests — I did protest, my lord — of secrecy and service, but she kissed me, as I live, of her own free accord — I trust your lordship conceives I did not act amiss."

Futelli had agreed to carry a letter to a man whom Levidolce intended to make her lover, although she had been having an affair with Lord Adurni. Also, she had kissed him, although she had been having an affair with Lord Adurni.

Futelli had violated Levidolce's privacy in bringing Lord Adurni her letter and telling him of their confidential conversation.

Futelli's loyalty was to Lord Adurni, not to Levidolce.

Futelli continued, "Please, rip off the seal of the letter and read it, my lord. You'll find sweet stuff, I dare believe."

Lord Adurni did not rip off the seal, but he did read out loud the superscription on the outside of the letter:

"*Present to the most accomplished of men, Malfato, with this love a service.*"

Lord Adurni then said, "Kind superscription! Please, find Malfato, and deliver this letter with compliments. Observe how ceremoniously — with how much respect — he receives it."

"Won't your lordship peruse the contents?" Futelli asked.

Lord Adurni said, "I have read enough, and I know too much."

It was obvious that this was a love letter: Levidolce was sexually interested in Malfato.

Lord Adurni added, "Be just and cunning: A wanton mistress is a common sewer."

Body fluids are dumped into a common sewer, and a different kind of body fluid is dumped into a common sexually available woman.

Lord Adurni continued, "A much newer project labors in my brain —"

He was planning something. Levidolce was his cast-aside lover. If she married Malfato, she would be happy and Lord Adurni would not have to worry about her.

Piero, Futelli's friend and another of Adurno's dependents, entered the room.

"Your friend!" Lord Adurni said. "Here's now the Gemini of wit."

Futelli and Piero were such friends that they were often together, and so they were metaphorically Gemini: twins.

Lord Adurni said, "What odd conceit is next on foot? Some trick of neat invention, ha, sirs?"

He suspected that they had a trick — a practical joke — in mind.

"A very fine trick, I do say, my lord," Piero replied.

"Your lordship's ear shall share in the plot," Futelli said.

"What is the plot?" Lord Adurni asked.

"You know, my lord," Piero said, "young Amoretta, old Trelcatio's daughter. He is an honest man, but poor."

"And, my good lord," Futelli said, "he who is honest must be poor, my lord: It is a common rule."

Lord Adurni was rich.

Lord Adurni said, "Well — Amoretta —"

Seeing that both Futelli and Piero were eager to speak, he said, "Please, speak one at a time. I know little about her — tell me more."

Futelli and Piero were Lord Adurni's dependents, and they did not want to get on his bad side. If he worried about them talking too much and interrupting, each wanted the other one to do the talking.

"Speak, Futelli," Piero said.

"Spare me," Futelli said. "Piero has a tongue that is more pregnant — ready and able to speak — than mine."

"Bah!" Piero said. "You are playing a trick on your fellow friend."

"The first one to speak shall be you," Futelli said.

"No, my good man," Piero said.

Lord Adurni said, "Well, keep your mirth, my dainty honeys; agree in the next two days who will do the talking. Until then —"

Piero said, "By any means, partake in the entertainment we have planned, my lord; this thing of youth —"

The "thing of youth" was young Amoretta, old Trelcatio's daughter.

Futelli interrupted, "— who is handsome enough; good face, quick eye, well-bred —"

Piero interrupted, "— is yet possessed so strangely —"

Futelli interrupted, "— with a humor of thinking she deserves —"

Piero interrupted, "— a duke, a count, at least a viscount, to be her husband, that —"

Futelli interrupted, "— she scorns all mention of a match beneath one of the foresaid nobles, and she will not ride in a caroche unless it is drawn by eight horses —"

A caroche is an Italian luxurious coach.

Piero interrupted, " — six she may be drawn to; four —"

Futelli interrupted, "— are for the poor. But as for two horses in a coach —"

Piero interrupted, "— she says they're not for creatures of Heaven's making; instead, they are fitter —"

Futelli interrupted, "— fitter for litters to convey hounds in than to convey Christian people, yet she herself —"

Piero interrupted, "— she herself walks always on foot, and does not know whether a coach does trot or amble —"

Futelli interrupted, "— except but by hearsay."

Amoretta was proud and felt that she deserved luxuries, but she had no experience of them, and so she did not know that coaches don't trot or amble — the horses pulling the coaches do the trotting or ambling.

Lord Adurni said, "Stop, gentlemen, you run a gallop. Both of you are out of breath, surely. It is a kind of compliment scarcely entered to the times, but certainly you coin a humor."

"Humors" are moods. Futelli and Piero were originals, and as such they were creating an original kind of comic duo.

Lord Adurni said, "Let me understand deliberately and systematically your idea for a trick."

Piero said, "In plain truth, my lord, the she whom we describe is such as we have described her, and she lives here, here in Genoa, this city, this very city, now, right now."

Lord Adurni asked, "Trelcatio's daughter?"

Futelli interrupted, "— has refused suitors of worthy rank, of substantial wealth, and of generous qualities only because they are not dukes or counts. Yet she herself with all her father's store of wealth can hardly weigh above four hundred ducats."

Lord Adurni said, "Now tell me your plan for entertainment."

"Without interruption and without delay," Piero said.

He described the practical joke: "Guzman, the Spaniard who was recently cashiered and is out of a job, is a man who most gravely observes the full punctilios, formalities, and niceties of his nation.

"Guzman the Spaniard is the man whom we have laid siege to, to convince to accost this she-piece — young Amoretta, old Trelcatio's daughter — under a pretense of being a grandee of Spain, and cousin to twelve princes."

A "piece" can be 1) a fortress, 2) a firearm, or 3) a woman.

Futelli said, "To be a rival to Guzman the Spaniard for Amoretta's love, we have engaged and enraged Fulgoso the Parvenu, the rich coxcomb — fool — who recently jumped into the status of a gentleman, despite coming out of the hut of a sutler — a seller of provisions to soldiers — in the recent Flemish wars."

The Flemish wars were the Thirty Years' War (1618-1648) between the Dutch and the Spaniards. Guzman was a Spaniard, and Fulgoso the Parvenu had Dutch ancestry from his mother's side, and so Guzman the Spaniard and Fulgoso the Parvenu would be rivals not just for Amoretta's love.

Futelli continued, "We have convinced Fulgoso the Parvenu that he is descended from Pantagruel of famous memory by the father's side."

Pantagruel was a giant in Rabelais' comic novel *Gargantua and Pantagruel*. He was the King of the Dipsodes. A dipsomaniac is an alcoholic.

Futelli continued, "And we have convinced Fulgoso the Parvenu that he is descended by the mother's side from Dame Fusti-Bunga, who, troubled for a long time with a strangury — a disease of the urinary tract — peed at last salt water so abundantly that she drowned the land between the Netherland towns of Zieriksee and Veere, where only steeples' tops are seen."

This part of the Netherlands had been flooded some years previously.

Dame Fusti-Bunga could possibly be Dame "Fusty-Bumga" or "Fusty Bum Ga," aka "Stinky Butt Go." *Ga* is Dutch for "go."

Or Dame Fusti-Bunga could possibly be Dame "Puffed-out Musty Wine Cask."

The adjective "bungy" means "protuberant."

The adjective "fusty" means "musty" and can refer to the smell of a wine cask.

Or the name could mean both.

Futelli continued, "He casts beyond the moon, and will be greater yet, in spite of Don Guzman the Spaniard."

Fulgoso the Parvenu was ambitious to be greater in society: He had set his sights beyond the moon.

"Don" is a Spanish title, one that Guzman the Spaniard had not earned.

Lord Adurni said, "To carry out this practical joke, you must abuse the maiden beyond amends."

This could turn out to be a very cruel practical joke on Amoretta.

Futelli objected, "Just give us permission to carry out the joke, my lord, and it may happen, in addition to giving us mirth, to work a reformation on the maiden. Her father's permission has already been granted, and his thanks promised to us. Our intentions are to cause harmless trials — harmless ordeals — for her."

Such a practical joke could cause Amoretta to become less proud and more practical.

Lord Adurni said, "I betray no secrets of such purpose. I will not reveal your practical joke to anyone, or stop it."

Piero and Futelli said, "We are your lordship's humblest servants."

They exited.

Aurelio and Malfato talked together in a room in Malfato's house.

Aurelio said, "A melancholy grounded and resolved, received into a habit argues love, or the deep impression of strong discontents."

Malfato could be melancholy because he was in love or because he was suffering from depression.

Aurelio continued, "In cases of these rarities, a friend upon whose faith and confidence we may vent with security our grief, often becomes the best physician, for even if we find no remedy, we cannot miss receiving some relief even if we don't find total comfort and happiness, and believe, Malfato, that it is an ease to disburden our souls of secret clogs, where they may find a rest in pity, though not in redress."

Talking to a friend can provide some comfort even if talking fails to provide a cure.

Malfato said, "Let all this sense be yielded to. Know that I realize that you are making sense."

Aurelio said, "Perhaps you regard what I say the common nature of a nosy curiosity."

"Not I, sir," Malfato said.

"Or that other private ends sift your retirements," Aurelio said.

Aurelio wondered whether Malfato thought that he was inquiring about Malfato's private life for a purpose that could benefit Aurelio.

"I don't think that, either," Malfato replied.

Futelli entered the room and said, "With your permission, Malfato, I was sent here to ask for your time for a word or two in private."

"You were sent to me!" Malfato said. "What is on your mind?"

"This letter will inform you," Futelli said, giving Malfato Levidolce's letter.

"Letter!" Malfato said.

As he read the superscription, he said, "What's this? What's here?"

"Are you speaking to me, sir?" Futelli asked.

"This is a splendid puzzle!" Malfato said. "I'll endeavor to unfold it."

Letters were folded, and the superscription was written on the outside of the letter. He also wanted to unfold — solve — the problem.

Malfato unfolded the letter and began to read it.

Aurelio asked Futelli, "How is Lord Adurni?"

"To be sure, he is in good health, sir," Futelli said.

Aurelio said, "He is a noble gentleman, in addition to being fortunate in his endeavors. The general opinion of him proclaims that he has courtesy, behavior, language, and every fair demeanor, and that he is an exemplary example for others.

"Titles of honor add not to his worth, who is himself an honor to his titles."

In other words, according to Aurelio's words, Lord Adurni was an exemplary man, and he would be an exemplary man even if he lacked the title of Lord; in fact, he brought honor to the title of Lord rather than the title of Lord bringing honor to him.

Malfato asked, "Do you know from where this letter comes?"

Laughing, Futelli said, "I do know."

He had brought the letter to Malfato from Levidolce — and from Lord Adurni.

"Do you laugh?" Malfato said. "Except that I must consider such people as you as being like spaniels to those who feed and clothe them, I would print thy panderism upon thy forehead."

Cocker spaniels fawn upon those who feed them, and dependents such as Futelli fawn upon those who feed and clothe them.

Malfato believed that Futelli was working as a kind of pander to Levidolce, whom he did not respect, and as a kind of pander for Lord Adurni, whom he believed was trying to get him to marry Levidolce.

Malfato said, "There!"

He threw the letter at him.

He then said, "Bear back that paper to the hell from whence it gave thee thy directions; tell this lord that he ventured on a foolish policy in aiming at creating a scandal for my blood — for me and my family lineage.

"The trick is childish, base — tell him that it is base!"

The first "base" could mean "base man" or "base trick."

Futelli said, "You wrong him."

"Be wise, Malfato," Aurelio advised.

Malfato said, "Tell him, I know this whore. She who sent this temptation was the wife to, and divorced from, his abused servant the poor Benazzi, who was senseless of the wrongs done to him, so that Madam Levidolce and Lord Adurni might revel in their sexual sports without control, secure, unchecked."

Malfato knew that Lord Adurni and Levidolce had had an affair.

Aurelio said, "You range too wildly now — you are too much inconsiderate."

Malfato replied, "I am a gentleman free-born — a gentleman from birth.

"I never wore the rags of any great man's looks, nor fed upon scraps left over from their meals; I never crouched to the offal of an office promised — reward for long service — and then missed."

Malfato had never had to be a dependent and seek favor from lords. He never had to wear the lord's used clothing, eat the lord's leftovers, or seek an office or position — a promotion — that would be promised to him but given to someone else.

He continued, "I read no difference between this huge, this monstrous big word 'lord' and the word 'gentleman,' more than how the title sounds; for all I know, the latter is as noble as the first, and I'm sure it is more ancient."

At this time, people could buy titles, but Malfato had been born a gentleman and so his father and probably other male ancestors had been gentlemen.

Aurelio said, "Let me tell you, then, that you are too bitter, and say you know not what: Make all men equals, and confound all course of order and of nature! This is madness."

Aurelio believed in an aristocracy and in varying levels of social status: A lord such as Lord Adurni ranked higher than a gentleman such as Malfato.

Malfato said, "My opinion is true, and I have reason to be mad. Reason, Aurelio, in accordance with my truth and hopes.

"This wit Futelli brings to me a suit of love from Levidolce: a woman, however masked in concealing privacy, who is reputed to be the Lord Adurni's pensioner at least."

A pensioner receives money from another person. Malfato was saying that Levidolce had been Lord Adurni's paid mistress.

Malfato continued, "Am I a husband picked out for a strumpet? For a cast-suit of bawdry?"

A "cast-suit" is cast-aside clothing. According to Malfato, Levidolce was Lord Adurni's cast-aside mistress.

Malfato continued, "Aurelio, put yourself in my position. You could ill digest the trial of a patience so unfit."

In other words, Aurelio would also hardly accept Levidolce as a wife.

"Be gone, Futelli!" Malfato said. "Leave! Do not reduce in harshness one syllable of what you have heard me say. Another trick like this may tempt a peace to rage. Report what I have said! Be gone! Leave!"

Futelli replied, "I shall report your answer."

He exited.

Malfato said, "What have I said or done to deserve to be treated like this! In colder, less angry blood, I do confess that nobility requires duty and love; it is a badge of virtue. By one's action, nobility is first acquired, and it is next in rank to anointed royalty.

"Wherein have I neglected distance between social classes, or forgotten observance to my superiors?

"Surely, my name was in the note mistaken. The letter was meant to be sent to someone else."

Aurelio said, "We will consider the meaning of this mystery."

"No, we need not do that," Malfato said. "Let them fear bondage who are slaves to fear. The sweetest freedom is an honest heart."

CHAPTER 2

— 2.1 —

Futelli and Guzman the Spaniard talked together on a street. Guzman, an out-of-work soldier, was the Spaniard whom Futelli was trying to convince that Amoretta loved him. Amoretta wanted to marry a man of high social class, and so Futelli called Guzman the Spaniard "Don," a Spanish honorary title. Despite being proud, Guzman the Spaniard was wearing ragged clothing.

Futelli advised Guzman in how to woo and marry Amoretta, using military terminology that Guzman, an ex-military man, would understand.

Futelli said, "Dexterity and sufferance, brave Don, are the engines that the pure politician must work with."

"We understand," Guzman the Spaniard said, using the majestic plural.

Futelli said, "In subtleties of war — I talk to you now in the language of your own occupation, your trade, or whatever term you prefer — to a soldier the ambush of an enemy by stratagem or downright cutting throats is all one and the same thing."

The main goal is to win, no matter how the victory is achieved.

"Most certainly," Guzman the Spaniard said. "Go on, proceed."

Futelli said, "By way of parallel, you drill or exercise your company — whichever term you prefer — before you draw into the field; so in the feats of courtship the first choice consists of thoughts, behavior, words, the set of looks, the posture of the beard, *beso las manos*, curtsies of the knee. The very hums and ha's, thumps and ay me's!"

"*Beso las manos*" is Spanish for "kissing of the hands," a form of courtly action. Hums and ha's are sighs. A lover might thump his heart and cry "ay, me!" or "woe is me!"

"We understand all this," Guzman the Spaniard said. "Advance."

He understood that the first choice of a lover is to behave in such a way that the loved one would fall in love with him. He would have to act the way a lover acts.

Futelli said, "Then next your enemy in face — your mistress, mark it — now you consult either to skirmish slightly — that's careless amours — or to enter battle.

Guzman would have to meet Amoretta face to face, and he would have to choose whether to move quickly or slowly. Should he indicate his interest in her with small gestures or make a full assault on her to gain her love?

"Then you fall to open treaty, or to work by secret spies or gold: here you corrupt the chambermaid, a fatal engine."

An open treaty would be Amoretta acknowledging that Guzman was her beau.

Guzman the Spaniard could bribe a chambermaid to give him access to Amoretta. An engine is something that can be used to help you achieve an objective.

Futelli continued, "Or you place there an ambuscado — that's a contract with some of her close relatives for half her portion."

Guzman the Spaniard could bribe some of Amoretta's close relatives to help him marry Amoretta in return for half of the dowry she would bring to him.

Futelli was ignoring the inconvenient fact that Amoretta's father had little wealth.

Futelli continued, "Or you offer a truce, and in the interim run upon slaughter, it is a noble treachery — that's swear and lie; steal her away, and to her throw your cap into the air and cry '*Victoria!*'"

The final way of achieving a lover's objective is to kidnap the loved one for a forced marriage. "*Victoria!*" is Spanish for "Victory!"

Futelli concluded, "The field's thine own, my Don, she's thine."

In other words, you, Guzman, will be successful in making Amoretta your wife.

Guzman the Spaniard said, "We do vouchsafe her."

He would grant her the privilege of being his wife.

"Hold her, then, fast," Futelli said.

Guzman the Spaniard said, "I will hold her as fast as the arms of strong imagination can hold her."

Futelli said, "No, she's skipped out of your hold; my imagination's eyes perceive that she does not endure the touch or scent of your war-worn clothing. It has suffered from excessive use."

Guzman the Spaniard was dressed in ragged, and stinky, military clothing.

Futelli added, "I forgot in my instructions to you to warn you about your clothing; therefore, my warlike Don, clothe speedily your imagination and give yourself a more courtly outside."

"It is soon done," Guzman the Spaniard said.

"As soon as said," Futelli said.

He thought, *You can quickly mention all the clothes thou have more than that walking-wardrobe that is on thy back.*

Guzman the Spaniard then began to itemize a wardrobe of rich clothing, which Futelli thought — or perhaps knew — was completely imaginary:

"Imagine first our rich mockado [woolen pile cloth that imitated silk velvet] doublet, with our cut cloth-of-gold sleeves, and our quellio [Spanish ruff].

"Our diamond-buttoned callamanco [wool from Flanders] hose.

"Our plume of ostrich, with the embroidered scarf that the Duchess Infantasgo rolled [wrapped] our arm in."

Futelli said, "Aye, this is splendid clothing indeed!"

Guzman the Spaniard continued itemizing rich clothing:

"Our cloak, whose cape is larded with pearls, which the Indian caciques [Native American leaders] presented to our countryman the famous conquistador De Cortez for ransom of his life [if it was his life that was being ransomed, he should have paid money to the Indian caciques]; rated in value at thirteen thousand pistolets [Spanish gold coins]; the reward of our achievement, when we rescued the Infanta [daughter of the King of Spain] from the boar in single duel, near the Austrian forest, with this rapier, this only, exact, naked, single rapier."

Futelli said, "Top and top-gallant brave!"

Top and top-gallant sails are used to give a ship extra speed.

"Brave" also meant splendid.

Futelli was praising (with perhaps more than a hint of sarcasm) both the bravery required in the exploits that Guzman had mentioned, and the cloak that Guzman was describing, and perhaps the rapier that Guzman was holding.

Guzman the Spaniard said, "We will appear before our Amoretta like the descendant of our ancestors."

Futelli said, "Imagine that what you said is so, and imagine that this rich suit of imagination is the apparel on your back already now."

He thought, *It is most probable that the splendid clothing you described is imaginary.*

He then said, "Here stands your Amoretta. Make your approach and court her."

Futelli was going to pretend to be Amoretta and let Guzman court him — that is, her.

Guzman the Spaniard began a speech of courtship:

"Luster of beauty, so that I do not frighten your tender soul with horror, we may descend to tales of peace and love, soft whispers that suit ladies' private rooms.

"For the thunder of cannon, roaring smoke and fire as if hell's mouth had vomited confusion, the clash of steel, the neighs of barbed steeds, wounds spouting blood, towns capering in the air, castles pushed down, and cities plowed with swords, become great Guzman the Spaniard's oratory best, who, though victorious — and during life he must be victorious — yet now he grants parley to thy smiles."

In Christopher Marlowe's *Tamburlaine the Great, Part 2*, Tamburlaine speaks of making towns caper — dance — in the air. Explosives would make the towns do that.

A parley is a meeting between enemies. Guzman regarded courtship as a battle.

Futelli said, "By God's foot, Don, you talk too big! You make Amoretta tremble. Do you not see it in your imagination? I do, as plainly as you saw the death of the Austrian boar.

"She would rather hear about feasting than about fighting. Take her that way."

To conquer her, talk to her about the things she wants to talk about.

Guzman the Spaniard took the advice and spoke the way he had been recommended to speak:

"Yes, we will feast. My queen, my empress, my saint shall taste no delicacies but what are dressed with costlier spices than the Arabian bird sweetens her funeral bed with."

The Arabian bird is the mythological Phoenix. It lived for 500 years, and then built and set on fire a nest containing Arabian spices, burning itself up. The Phoenix was reborn from the ashes and lived for another 500 years before repeating the process.

Guzman the Spaniard continued, "We will riot with every course of foods, which may renew our blood into a spring, so pure, so high, that from our pleasures shall proceed a race of scepter-bearing princes, who at once must reign in every quarter of the globe."

Futelli thought, *Can more be said by one who feeds on herring and garlic constantly?*

Guzman the Spaniard continued, "Yes, we will feast —"

"Enough!" Futelli said. "She's taken, and she will love you now as well in your military clothing as she would love you in your imagined splendid clothing.

"Your dainty ten-times-dressed leather military jacket, with this language you used just now, bold man of arms, shall win her, don't doubt it, much better than shall silken puppetry — artifice and pretense."

Dressed leather has received further preparation after being tanned.

Futelli continued:

"Think no more about your 'mockadoes, callamancoes, quellios, pearl-larded capes, and diamond-buttoned breeches.'

"Leave such poor outside helps to whining lovers such as Fulgoso, your weak rival, is — that emaciated-brained companion.

"You must appear, at first, at least, in your own warlike fashion — so I advise you — and don't change a thread about you. While courting, wear the same clothing you are wearing now."

Guzman the Spaniard said, "My inclination is to take your advice; for I, sir, am a man who does not often change his clothing. I will do as you advise."

Futelli said, "Why, and by so doing, you will carry her from all the world. I'm proud my stars designed me to be an instrument in such a high employment. I'm glad that it is my fate to advise you how to win Amoretta."

Guzman the Spaniard replied, "Gravely spoken. You may be proud of your fate."

Fulgoso the Parvenu and Piero appeared. Futelli had been persuading Guzman to woo Amoretta; Piero had been persuading Fulgoso the Parvenu, a wealthy but unintelligent young dandy who had suddenly experienced a rise in wealth and social status. Unlike Guzman, Fulgoso the Parvenu was very well dressed indeed.

Fulgoso the Parvenu, who had been gambling, said, "What is lost is lost, money is trash, and ladies are et-ceteras, play's play, luck's luck, fortune's an I-know-what."

Fulgoso the Parvenu did not mind thinking bad language, but he did not want to say it out loud. Readers can guess that he thinks lowly about women, including Lady Fortune. Later, he will refer to women as "flirts and flighty puffballs."

He continued, "You see the worst of me, and — what's all this now?"

He had caught sight of Futelli and Guzman.

Piero was not ready to meet the others; he wanted to have fun at Fulgoso the Parvenu's expense before having fun at the expense of both Fulgoso the Parvenu and Guzman the Spaniard; therefore, he deliberately mistook "What's all this now?" to be asking "Who is Fulgoso the Parvenu now?"

Piero answered the question by praising Fulgoso the Parvenu: "A very spark, I vow, a witty young man: You will be called Fulgoso the Invincible! But did the fair Spinella lose an equal part in gambling? How much in all, do you say?"

Fulgoso the Parvenu answered, "Barely threescore — sixty — ducats, thirty ducats apiece. We need not care who knows it. She played; I joined my half to her half, walked by after we lost, and whistled after my usual manner like this" — he whistled — "unmoved, as if no such thing had ever been, as it were, although I saw the winners share my money. His lordship and an honest gentleman put it in their moneybags, but not as merrily as I whistled it off."

He whistled again.

"A noble confidence!" Piero said.

On the other side of the street, Futelli said to Guzman the Spaniard, "Do you see your rival?"

Guzman the Spaniard answered, "With contempt I do."

Fulgoso the Parvenu then said to Piero, "I can forgo things nearer than my gold — things allied to my affections and my blood. Yes, I can forgo honor, as it were, with the same kind of careless confidence, and come off fairly, too, as it were."

Piero said, "But you cannot forgo your love, Fulgoso."

Fulgoso the Parvenu replied, "No, she's inherent, and my own past losing."

His love, he believed, was Amoretta, and she was firmly fixed — inherent — in his heart.

Occasionally, Piero mocked Fulgoso's catchphrase — "as it were" — by using it.

Piero said, "It tickles me to think with how much state you, as it were, did run at tilt in love before your Amoretta."

The image was of two jousters galloping at full tilt toward each other in competition to see who can knock the other off his or her horse.

Fulgoso the Parvenu said, "Broke my lance."

Piero held in his laughter as he imagined that Amoretta had broken Fulgoso's penis, but he said, "Of wit! Of wit!"

If Amoretta had broken Fulgoso's lance of wit — that is, intelligence — she had captured his love. Because of love, or "love," Fulgoso lacked the intelligence to know that she had some serious flaws.

Fulgoso the Parvenu said, "I mean so, as it were, and laid flat on her back — both the horse and the woman."

Piero said, "Right, as it were."

Fulgoso the Parvenu replied, "What else, man, as it were?"

Futelli and Guzman the Spaniard walked over to Piero and Fulgoso the Parvenu. They had heard Fulgoso say that he had knocked Amoretta on her back.

If he had done that, she would be in the missionary-sex position.

Guzman asked Fulgoso, "Did you do this to her? Do you dare to boast about your triumph, with us present? Huh?"

Fulgoso the Parvenu whistled the Spanish Pavane, a slow, stately dance.

Futelli asked Guzman, "What do you think, Don, about this brave man?"

"A man!" Guzman the Spaniard said, scornfully. "It is some bundle of reeds, or empty cask in which the wind with whistling entertains itself."

Futelli, Guzman's advocate, said to Fulgoso, "Bear up, sir; he's your rival; budge from him not an inch; your grounds are honor."

Piero, Fulgoso's advocate, said to Guzman, "Stoutly ventured. Don, hold him to it."

Fulgoso the Parvenu said, "I agree, a fine idea, a very fine idea — and thus I told her that, for my own part, if she liked me, so! If not, not; 'for, my duck, or doe,' said I, 'it is no fault of mine that I am noble. Grant that another may be noble, too. And then we're both one noble — better still!

"Hit or miss, good sir, close her eyes and choose; if one must have her, the other goes without her — best of all!

"My spirit is too high to fight for a woman, and I am too full of mercy to be angry. This is a foolish generous quality from which no might of man can beat me, I'm resolved."

Guzman the Spaniard said, "Have thou a spirit, then, ha? Does thy weapon speak the language of Toledo, of Bilboa, or of dull Pisa? If it is an Italian blade or Spanish metal, be brief. We challenge you to answer."

Futelli said, "Famous Don!"

Fulgoso the Parvenu said, "What does it talk? My weapon speaks no language. It is a Dutch iron truncheon."

"Dutch!" Guzman the Spaniard said.

At this time, the Dutch and the Spaniards regarded each other as enemies.

Fulgoso the Parvenu said, "And, if need be, it will maul one's hide, in spite of who says nay."

Guzman the Spaniard said, "Dutch to a Spaniard! Hold me!"

In other words: Futelli, hold me back so I don't fight him here and now.

"Hold me, too, sirrah, if thou are my friend, for I love no fighting," Fulgoso the Parvenu said to Piero. "Yet hold me, lest in pity I fly off. If I must fight, I must; in a scurvy quarrel I defy hes and shes: twit me with Dutch!

"Hang Dutch and French, hang Spanish and Italians, Christians and Turks. Rubbish, all's one to me!

"I know what's what, I know on which side my bread is buttered."

Guzman the Spaniard said, "Buttered! Dutch again!"

The Dutch had an international reputation for liking butter.

He added, "You come not with intention to affront us?"

Fulgoso the Parvenu said, "Front me no fronts; if thou are angry, squabble — here's my defense, and thy destruction."

He whistled the sound that ordered an army to charge.

He added, "If we are friends, shake hands, and go with me to dinner."

Using the majestic plural, Guzman the Spaniard said, "We will embrace the proposal; it does relish. The cavaliero treats on terms of honor. Peace is not to be balked on fair conditions."

"Still Don is Don the Great," Futelli said.

"He shows the greatness of his vast stomach in his quick embracement of the other's dinner," Piero said.

"It was the ready means to catch his friendship," Futelli said.

Piero said to Guzman the Spaniard and Fulgoso the Parvenu, "You are a pair of Worthies who make the Nine no wonder."

The Nine Worthies were nine great men: three from the Bible, three from classical times, and three from romances.

The three from the Bible were Joshua, King David, and Judas Maccabaeus.

The three from classical times were Hector of Troy, Alexander the Great, and Julius Caesar.

The three from romances were King Arthur, Holy Roman Emperor Charlemagne, and the French Crusader Godfrey of Bouillon.

Guzman the Spaniard and Fulgoso the Parvenu were not more wonderful than the Nine Worthies.

Futelli said, "Now, since fate ordains that one of two must be the man, the man of men who must enjoy alone love's darling, Amoretta, each of you will take the liberty to show himself before her, without the cross of interruption of one from the other. He whose sacred mystery of earthly blessings crowns the pursuit and wins Amoretta to be his wife, be happy!"

Piero said, "And until then live as brothers in society."

Guzman the Spaniard said, "We are fast."

He meant: Fulgoso and I are fast friends.

Fulgoso the Parvenu said, "I vow a match. I'll feast the Don today, and fast with him tomorrow."

Guzman the Spaniard said, "These are fair conditions."

Guzman was unlikely to have the money to pay for a feast.

Lord Adurni, Spinella, Amoretta, and Castanna walked down the street.

Lord Adurni ordered, "Futelli and Piero, follow us speedily."

Piero replied, "My lord, we serve you."

Futelli said to Fulgoso the Parvenu and Guzman the Spaniard, "We shall soon return."

Everyone except Fulgoso the Parvenu and Guzman the Spaniard exited.

Fulgoso the Parvenu said, "What's that I saw? A sound."

"A voice for certain," Guzman the Spaniard said.

"It named a lord," Fulgoso the Parvenu said.

Guzman the Spaniard said, "Here are lords, too, we take it. We carry blood about us as rich and haughty as any of the Twelve Caesars."

Suetonius' *The Lives of the Twelve Caesars* contained biographies of the Roman Emperors from Julius Caesar to Domitian. Many of the stories Suetonius told about the twelve Roman Emperors were scurrilous. In some English translations, the most shocking stories were not translated, but were left in the original Latin and placed in an appendix.

Fulgoso the Parvenu said, "Gulls or Moguls; tag-rag or other; *hogen mogen van den*, skipjacks, or *chiauses*."

Gulls are fools. Moguls are heads of a historical Muslim dynasty.

Tag-rag is the rabble or riff-raff.

"*Hogen mogen van den*" are Dutch words meaning, roughly, "of the high mightinesses." Skipjacks are whipper-snappers. "*Chiauses*" are Turkish messengers.

Fulgoso contrasted the high and the low.

He then said, "Whoo! The brace are flinched; in other words, the pair of shavers — swindlers — has sneaked away from us, Don!"

Fulgoso knew that Futelli and Piero were not good people. They had not hidden their mockery enough for him not to pick up on it. That was one reason why he had sought Guzman's friendship.

Fulgoso then asked, "Why, what are we!"

Guzman the Spaniard replied, "The valiant will stand up to it."

He was willing to resist Futelli and Piero.

Fulgoso the Parvenu said, "So say I; we will eat and drink and squander, until all do split again."

The verb "split" meant "suffer a shipwreck." They would eat, drink, and be merry until something bad happened, or until they split apart and went off in different directions.

Guzman the Spaniard said, "March on with greediness."

They went off to feast together.

Martino and Levidolce met in a room in Martino's house. Martino was Levidolce's great-uncle, and he was concerned about his great-niece's bad reputation. The general tongue — general opinion — was that she had had an affair with Lord Adurni.

Martino said, "You cannot answer what a general tongue objects against your folly. I may curse the interest you lay claim to in my blood — I may curse because you are related to me.

"Your mother, my dear great-niece, died, I thought, too soon, but she is happy; had she lived until now and known the vanities your life has dealt in, she would have wished herself into an early grave."

Levidolce replied, "Sir, consider my sex. If I were a man, my sword would get revenge for my wounded honor, and reprieve my name from injury, by printing some deadly character on the bosoms of those whose drunken excesses vomit such base aspersions against me."

In other words, if she were a man, she would fight duels with the men who maliciously gossiped about her.

She continued, "As I am a woman, my scorn and contempt of them is virtuous; what I deserve stands far above their malice."

In her case, showing only her scorn and contempt of them is virtuous because if she were a man she would duel with them and kill them.

Martino said, "Levidolce, hypocrisy puts on a holy robe, yet never changes its nature. Remember how in your girl's days, you fell truly in love and married. You married — pay attention now — whom?

"A trencher-waiter!"

He added, sarcastically, "Shrewd preferment!"

A trencher-waiter brings plates of food to the dining table of his master. It is a low-status job.

Martino continued, "But your childhood then excused that fault; for similarly footmen have run away with lusty heirs, and stable-grooms have reached to some fair-ones' personal chambers."

Levidolce said, "Please let me not be bandied with and talked about, sir, and baffled and disgraced by your intelligence."

The intelligence was the information he had heard about her.

"So, you are touched to the quick!" Martino said. "Fine mistress, I will, then, make known at length the progress of your infamy.

"On pretense of disagreement, you must be divorced from your husband. In fact, you were divorced from him, and I must pretend to support the reasons.

"On better hopes, moreover, I took you home, provided you with my care, justified your alteration in marital status, and took delight in entertaining such visitants of worth and rank as tendered civil respects, but then, even then —"

"What then?" Levidolce asked. "Sweet grand-uncle, do not spare me."

Martino said, "I am more ashamed to fear that my hospitality acted like that of a bawd — and to give it that name — to your unchaste desires, than you are ashamed to hear and know it."

"Whose whore am I?" Levidolce asked. "For that's your plainest meaning."

Martino said, "If you were modest, the word you uttered — 'whore' — would at last force a blush from you.

"Lord Adurni is a bounteous lord. It is said that he parts with gold and jewels like a free and liberal purchaser. He wriggles into ladies' pleasures by a right of pension: He gives them gold and jewels."

He then said sarcastically, "But you know nothing about this."

He continued, "You have grown to be a topic of tavern talk and subject matter for fiddlers' songs. I toil to build up the reputation of my family, and you toil to pluck up the foundation.

"Just this morning, before the common-council, young Malfato — who had been summoned on account of some lands he held, supposed to belong to certain orphans — as I questioned his tenure of the land in particulars, he answered that my worship needed not to flaw his right, for if the mood held him, he could make a jointure to my over-living and over-loving great-niece without being financially oppressed."

A jointure is wealth settled on a wife to support her in case her husband dies first.

Apparently, Malfato was the custodian of land belonging to some orphans until they reached legal age. By mentioning the jointure, he was making the point that he had enough money that he need not cheat the orphans. He was also hinting that Levidolce wanted to marry him.

Martino continued, "He told me to tell her, too, that she was a kind young soul, and might in time be wooed by a loving man, without doubt."

He then said, sarcastically, "Here was a jolly breakfast!"

Levidolce replied, "Uncles are privileged more than our parents; some wise man in civic affairs has rectified, no doubt, your knowledge, sir.

"After all the discussion about public business had been completed — then, for lack of other things to talk about, I by chance came to be the topic of grave discourse, but, by your leave, I would rather wish to earn my bread from a stranger's table than be given bread from a friend's table if I had to be daily subjected to the friend's unfitting rebukes."

Martino said, "Come, come, get to the point."

Levidolce said, "May all the curses due to a ravisher of sober truth dam up the graceless mouths of those false accusers!"

Martino said, "Now you become out of control, just in the wenches' trim and garb — the usual style of wanton women. These 'prayers' speak your 'devotions' purely."

Crying, Levidolce replied, "Sir, alas, what would you have me do? I have no orators, other than my tears, to plead my innocence, since you forsake me and are pleased to lend an open ear against my honest fame.

"I wish all their spite could harass all my contentment and turn it into a desperate ruin!

"Oh, dear goodness! There is a right for wrongs."

"There is," Martino said, "but first sit in commission on your own defects. Accuse yourself; be your own jury, judge, and executioner. I take no pleasure in my vexation."

Levidolce said, "All the short remains of undesired life shall only speak the extremity of penance; your opinion enjoins it, too."

She was promising to repent her sins for the rest of her short, unwanted life.

Martino said, "Enough; thy tears prevail against credulity."

His words were ambiguous. Do her tears prevail against belief in her reform? In that case, he did not believe her repentance was sincere. Or do her tears prevail against belief in what people have said about her? In that case, he did not believe what people have said about her.

Levidolce said, "My miseries, as in a mirror, present me the torn face of an unguided youth."

In ancient Greece and Rome, grief-stricken women would scratch their faces with their fingernails.

Martino said, "No more."

Trelcatio entered the room, carrying a letter that he had opened and read.

"Trelcatio!" Martino said. "Some business speeds you here."

Trelcatio said, "Happy news — signor Martino, give me your ear, please."

He drew him away so that Levidolce could not hear them.

Trelcatio then said, "My nephew Auria has done brave service; and I hear — let's be exceedingly private — that he has returned high in the Duke of Florence's respects. It is said — but say no words about this — that he has soundly defeated and knocked about the despicable Turks."

Martino asked, "Why would you have his merits so unknown? Why not let everyone know about his success?"

Trelcatio said, "I have not yet fully confirmed this news. Withdraw with me, and you shall read all that this paper talks about."

Martino said, "I see!"

He then said, "Levidolce, you know what I think. Be cheerful."

He then said, "Come, Trelcatio."

He added, "Causes of joy or grief do seldom happen without companions near. Thy resolutions have given another birth to my contentment."

The word "resolutions" was ambiguous.

If he had believed Levidolce's resolution to reform, that would make him happy.

But another meaning of "resolution" was "an explanatory account" (*Oxford English Dictionary*). Trelcatio's explanatory account of Auria's victory would certainly make him happy.

Possibly, Martino believed both Levidolce's resolution and Trelcatio's explanatory account, aka resolution.

Martino and Trelcatio exited.

Levidolce said to herself, "Even so, wise great-uncle! Much good may it do you!

"I have been discovered!"

People had learned about her affair with Lord Adurni, and they probably knew that she had pursued Malfato.

She continued, "I could fly out and mix vengeance with my love — unworthy man, Malfato!

"My good lord, my hot in blood, splendid lord, grows cold toward me, too!"

She was talking about Lord Adurni.

She continued, "Well, raise dotage — excessive love — into rage, and sleep no longer. Affection turned to hatred threatens evil."

Piero, Amoretta, Futelli, and Castanna talked together in an apartment in Lord Adurni's house. Amoretta lisped. She pronounced S's and T's as "Th."

Piero said, "In the next gallery you may behold such living pictures, lady, such rich pieces of kings and queens and princes, that you'd think that they breathe and smile upon you."

Amoretta said, "Have they crownths, great crownths oth gold upon their headths?"

"Crowns of pure gold," Piero said, "Drawn all in state."

Amoretta asked, "How many horthes, please tell me, are ith their chariots?"

She meant to ask how many horses "pull their chariots," not how many horses "are is [or possibly, *with*, pronounced *'ith*] their chariots."

Piero answered, "Sixteen, some twenty."

"My sister!" Castanna said, referring to Spinella. "Why have we left her alone? Where is she staying, gentlemen?"

Futelli said, "She is viewing the rooms: It is likely that you'll meet her in the gallery. This house is full of curiosities very fit for ladies' sights."

Amoretta said, "Yeth, yeth, the thight of pwinthes ith a fine thight."

"Good," Castanna said. "Let's find her."

Piero said, "Sweet ladies, go this way."

He whispered to Futelli, "See that the doors are secure."

"Don't worry," Futelli whispered back. "I will."

In another room in Lord Adurni's house, Lord Adurni and Spinella were alone together. A banquet was set out on a table.

Nearby but out-of-sight singers sang these lyrics:

"Pleasures, beauty, youth attend ye

"Whiles the spring of nature lasteth;

"Love and melting thoughts attend ye;

"Use the time, ere winter hasteth.

"Active blood and free delight.

"Place and privacy invite.

"Do, do! Be kind as fair;

"Lose not opportunity for air.

"She is cruel that denies it.

"Bounty best appears in granting;

"Stealth of sport as soon supplies it,

"Whiles the dues of love are wanting.

"Here's the sweet exchange of bliss,

"When each whisper proves a kiss.

"In the game are felt no pains,

"For in all the loser gains."

The song was about *carpe diem*: Seize the day.

The references to spring and winter advised the hearer to make good use of youth.

It could also be interpreted as a song of seduction.

The word "do" meant "have sex," and the words "Do, do" appeared in the song.

The word "air" in this context meant "gossip," and the lyric *"Lose not opportunity for air"* could be interpreted "Don't lose an opportunity for sex because you are worried about gossip."

It also referred to sex as "win-win" entertainment: *"In the game are felt no pains / For in all the loser gains."*

Lord Adurni said, "Plead not, fair creature, without sense of so uncompassionately against a service faulty in nothing more than pure obedience."

Spinella had let him know that she did not want to be alone with him.

Lord Adurni continued, "My honors and my fortunes are led captives in triumph by your all-commanding beauty, and if you ever felt the power of love, the rigor of an uncontrolled passion, the tyranny of thoughts, consider mine, in some proportion, by the strength of yours. Thus may you yield and conquer."

Spinella replied, "Do not study, my lord, to apparel folly in the weed of costly colors."

She was probably convinced that he was attempting to seduce her despite her marriage, and she did not want him to dress up his attempt with flattery. It would be more honest to speak openly. By referring to the seduction attempt as "folly," however, she was making it clear that she preferred no attempt at seduction.

She continued, "Henceforth cast off far from your noblest nature the contempt of goodness, and be gentler to your reputation, by purchase of a life to grace your story."

She wanted him to turn away from evil and embrace good as a way to lead a life that would enhance his reputation.

Lord Adurni said, "Dear, how sweetly reproof drops from that balmy spring, your breath!

"Now I could read a lecture of my griefs, unearth a mine of jewels at your foot, command a golden shower to rain down, impoverish every kingdom of the East that traffics in richest clothes and silks, if you would grant me one mild, temperate scolding to my riot."

When Zeus, king of the gods, wished to seduce Danaë, he turned himself into a shower of gold and gained entrance into her private chamber.

Lord Adurni continued, "Otherwise, such a sacrifice — offering to a deity — can but give birth to suspicion of returns to my devotion in mercenary blessings; for that saint to whom I vow myself must never lack fit offerings to her altar."

If Spinella did not criticize him, people might suspect that any gifts he gave her would result in her giving "mercenary blessings" such as sexual favors to him in return for his gifts. This is what Martino suspected had happened between Lord Adurni and Levidolce.

In an apostrophe to her husband, who was not present, Spinella said, "Auria, Auria, don't fight for a reputation abroad; but come, my husband — fight for thy wife at home!"

Lord Adurni said, "Oh, never rank, dear cruelty, one who is sworn your creature among your country's enemies."

Lord Adurni was sworn Spinella's "creature" — he was her servant.

He continued, "I use no force but humble words, delivered from a tongue that's secretary — confidant — to my heart."

Spinella said, "How poorly some, tame to their wild desires, fawn on abuse of virtue! Please, my lord, don't make your house my prison."

Lord Adurni said, "Grant a freedom to him who is the bondman — servant — to your beauty."

A noise sounded, and the door was forced open.

Aurelio, Auria's friend, ran into the room, followed by Castanna, Amoretta, Futelli, and Piero.

Aurelio said to Castanna, Amoretta, Futelli, and Piero, "Keep back, you secret contrivers of false pleasures, or I shall force you back."

He then said to Lord Adurni and Spinella, "Can it be possible? Locked in a room together, and alone, too!"

He added sarcastically, "Chaste hospitality! A banquet in a bed-chamber!"

He then said, "Lord Adurni, you are a dishonorable man!"

Lord Adurni replied, "What do you, rude man, see that can broach scandal here? There is nothing scandalous here."

Aurelio said to Lord Adurni, "I have more to say to you hereafter."

He then said to Spinella, "Oh, woman, who has lost every good report about thyself, thy wronged Auria has come home with glory!"

He was convinced that she was guilty of at least of wanting to have an affair with Lord Adurni.

Aurelio continued, "Prepare a welcome to uncrown the greatness of his prevailing fates."

Auria thought that he was riding high on the wheel of Lady Fortune, but news of his wife's behavior here would bring him low.

Spinella said, "While you, most likely, are furnished with some news for entertainment, which must become your friendship, to be knit more fast between your souls by my removal both from his heart and memory!"

She believed that he was ruining her marriage so that he could become better friends with her husband.

Lord Adurni said, "This is a rich conquest, to triumph on a lady's injured reputation, without a proof or any warrant!"

Futelli asked Aurelio, "Have I life, sir? Faith? Christianity?"

Futelli was willing to back up Lord Adurni; so was Piero.

Piero said, "Put me on the rack, on the wheel, or in the galleys, if —"

He had mentioned three punishments: 1) people were stretched on the rack until their joints painfully separated, 2) people were tied to a wheel and their bones broken, or people were restrained on the ground and a heavy breaking wheel was dropped on them to break their bones, and 3) people were sentenced to row in galley-ships as slaves.

Aurelio interrupted, "Silence, you two agents in the merchandise of scorn! Your sounds are deadly."

"Agents in the merchandise of scorn" are pimps.

He then said to Spinella's sister, "Castanna, I could pity your consent to such ignoble practice, but I find coarse fortunes easily seduced, and herein all claim to goodness ceases."

He believed that Castanna had helped her sister to be alone with Lord Adurni for immoral activities, and therefore she had lost any claim to goodness.

"Show your tyrannous behavior," Castanna said.

"What is in store for me?" Spinella said. "Out with it!"

Aurelio replied, "Horror and fearful suffering that are suitable for such a forfeit of obedience."

In this society, wives were expected to be obedient to their husbands — that included being faithful to them.

He continued, "Don't hope that any falsity in friendship can palliate a broken faith; it dares not."

Having an affair with a friend does *not* mitigate unfaithfulness.

He continued, "Plead in thy prayers, fair, vow-breaking wanton woman, to dress thy soul anew, whose purer whiteness is sullied by thy change from truth to folly.

"A fearful storm is hovering; it will fall. No shelter can avoid it. Let the guilty sink under their own ruin."

He exited.

Spinella said, "How unmanly his anger threatens evil against us!"

Amoretta asked, "Whom, I ask, does the man speak to?"

Lord Adurni said to Spinella, "Lady, don't be angry; I will stand as champion for your honor, and I will risk all that is dearest to me."

Spinella said, "Mercy, heaven! *He* will be champion for me!"

She added, "And with Auria living! Auria! Auria lives, and Auria is my champion, and I have my innocence for my guard. As free as are my husband's clearest thoughts, my innocence shall keep off vain misconstructions of my actions.

"I must beg your charities; sweet sister, yours, to leave me and let me be alone. I need no companions now.

"Let me appear as my own lawyer and speak to my husband privately.

"The alternative is to let me appear in open court — like some forsaken client. Let me be cast into an open court to plead my case in public because of a lack of honest plea — oh, misery!"

She wanted to talk to her husband privately. Being made to appear in an open court to plead her case should happen only if she were guilty.

She exited.

Lord Adurni said, "Her resolution's violent — let's quickly follow her."

He was afraid that she would commit suicide.

Castanna said, "By no means, sir. You've followed her already, I fear. With too much ill success in trial of unbecoming courtesies, your welcome ends in so sad a farewell."

Lord Adurni said, "I will endure the roughness of the encounter like a gentleman, and I will escort you to your homes, whatever happens to me."

CHAPTER 3

— 3.1 —

Fulgoso the Parvenu and Guzman the Spaniard talked together on the street in front of Martino's house.

Fulgoso the Parvenu said, "I say, Don, brother of mine, win her and wear her. And so will I. If it should be my luck to lose her, I lose a pretty wench, and there's the worst of it."

"Win her and wear her" meant "win her and consummate the marriage."

The word "wench" can be used affectionately, but Guzman the Spaniard regarded it as being negative.

Guzman the Spaniard objected, "'Wench,' said ye? Most mechanically, bah! 'Wench' is your trull, your blowse, your dowdy."

A trull is a whore, a blowse is a male beggar's female significant other, and a dowdy is a shabbily dressed woman.

He added, "But, sir brother, he who names my queen of love without his hat taken off, or without his saying grace as if he were at some paranymphal — wedding — feast, is rude and is not versed in literature. Dame Amoretta, lo, I am thy sworn champion!"

Fulgoso the Parvenu said, "So am I, too. I can, if needed, if she turns scurvy, unswear myself again, and never change colors."

"Never change colors" meant that he could unswear his vow to be her champion without blushing.

If it also meant that he could unswear his vow to be her champion without changing his allegiance, then his oath to be her champion was worthless.

He added, "Pish, man! The best — although we call them ladies, madams, fairs, fines, and honeys — are only flesh and blood, and now and then, too, when the fit's come on them, they will prove themselves to be just flirts and flighty puffballs."

Guzman the Spaniard said, "Our choler must advance."

If he was using the majestic plural, he meant that his anger against Fulgoso must make him — Guzman — work for a better position in regards to the object of their affection: the lisping Amoretta.

If he was using "our" to mean "his and Fulgoso's," he meant that their anger at each other must make them physically fight.

Fulgoso the Parvenu asked, "Do you long for a beating? Shall we try a slash? Here's something that shall do it" — he drew his sword.

He then said, referring to Guzman's head as if it were a cask, "I'll tap a gallon of thy brains, and fill thy hogshead with two of wine for it."

Guzman the Spaniard said, "Not in friendship, brother."

Fulgoso the Parvenu said, "Or I will whistle thee into an fever.

"Hang it. Let's be sociable. Let's drink until we roar and scratch, and then drink ourselves asleep again — the fashion! Thou do not know the fashion."

Fulgoso was referring to a fashionable way of behaving.

For roaring boys, the fashion was to get drunk, cause trouble, and then drink again until they slept.

For male lovers, the fashion was to orate a poetic blazon — a catalog of female beauties — to and/or about the loved one.

To show that he knew the fashion for male lovers, Guzman the Spaniard said, "Her fair eyes,

"Like [Similar] to a pair of pointed beams drawn from

"The sun's most glorious orb, do dazzle sight

"Audacious to gaze there; then over those

"A several bow of jet securely twines

"In semicircles; under them two banks

"Of roses red and white, divided by

"An arch of polish'd ivory, surveying

"A temple from whence oracles proceed

"More gracious than Apollo's, more desir'd

"Than amorous songs of poets softly tun'd."

The song poetically described the parts of a lady's face.

The "several bow of jet … / In semicircles" are the lady's eyebrows.

The "two banks / Of roses red and white" are her cheeks.

"An arch of polish'd ivory" is her nose.

The "temple from whence oracles proceed" is her mouth.

Oracles are prophecies; Apollo was the god of prophecy.

Fulgoso the Parvenu said, "Hey! What's this?"

Guzman the Spaniard continued, "Oh, but those other parts. All —"

Guzman seemed about to describe Amoretta's lady parts.

Fulgoso the Parvenu interrupted, "All! Stop there. I bar play under board."

In this culture, the word "board" can mean a table. When sitting at a table, Amoretta's waist and lower parts would be under the table.

He continued, "My part yet lies therein."

This sentence contained sexual punning. His sexual "part" would be lying in some part of Amoretta that would be under the table while she sat there.

Fulgoso continued, "You never saw the things you sketch thus."

Guzman the Spaniard said, "But I have dreamt of every part about her, and I can lay open her several inches as exactly — pay attention — as if I had took measure with a compass, a rule, or a yard, from head to foot."

Her "several inches" could refer to her height, or to the depth of her vagina. The word "yard" sometimes meant "penis."

Fulgoso said, "Oh, splendid! And all this in a dream!"

Guzman the Spaniard said, "A very dream."

A very wet dream.

Fulgoso the Parvenu said, "My waking brother soldier has been turned into a sleeping carpenter or tailor, which goes for half a man."

Carpenters and tailors — and Guzman — took measurements.

Benazzi, dressed as an outlaw, appeared.

Levidolce appeared at a window above.

Benazzi and Levidolce had been married, but they had divorced.

Seeing Benazzi, Fulgoso said, "Who's he? Bear up!"

Benazzi the Outlaw said, "Death of a good reputation, the wheel, strappado, galleys, rack, are ridiculous fopperies — goblins to frighten babies. Poor lean-souled rogues! They will swoon at the scar of a pin; one tear dropped from their harlot's eyes breeds earthquakes in their bones."

The strappado was a torture in which the victim's arms were tied behind him and then he was lifted into the air by that rope.

Futelli the Parvenu said, "Bless us! A monster, patched of dagger-bombast."

Bombast is padding worn in clothing. Benazzi's "padding" consisted of daggers.

Futelli continued, "His eyes are like copper basins, and he has exchanged hair with a shaggy dog."

Guzman the Spaniard said, "Let us, then, avoid him, or stand upon our guard — the foe approaches."

Benazzi the Outlaw said, "Cutthroats by the score abroad, come home and rot in fripperies."

Benazzi had been a cutthroat — actually a soldier — abroad. Many soldiers who returned from wars abroad would become outlaws or beggars to make a living. They often were hungry and often wore old, ragged clothing, aka fripperies.

Benazzi the Outlaw continued talking about the options open to a discharged soldier:

"Brave man-at-arms, go turn pander, do."

A pander is a pimp.

He continued, "Stalk for a mess of warm broth — damnable!"

A "mess" in this context is a meal. The word "stalk" can mean "walk stealthily." A robber could stalk a man to rob him and get money for a meal.

The word "stalk" can also mean "march proudly." Soldiers can march through a territory to earn their meals.

Benazzi the Outlaw continued, "Honorable cuts are only badges for a fool to boast about."

What is the worth of a scar honorably earned in battle? Not much.

He continued, "The raw-ribbed apothecary poisons *cum privilegio*, and is paid."

"Raw-ribbed" means "with ribs showing." The apothecary in Shakespeare's *Romeo and Juliet* is starving and so is willing to sell Romeo poison although doing so is a capital crime.

The apothecary sells the poison "*cum privilegio*," which is Latin for "with privilege" or "by right." The raw-ribbed apothecary has the natural right to do what it takes to get food to eat to stay alive.

Benazzi the Outlaw continued, "Oh, the commonwealth of beasts is most politicly ordered!"

"Politicly" can mean 1) according to law, and/or 2) shrewdly and skillfully.

Benazzi the Outlaw would soon criticize the commonwealth of beasts, but he could also criticize the commonwealth of men.

Guzman the Spaniard said to Fulgoso, "Brother, we'll keep aloof; there is no valor in tugging with a man-fiend."

Fulgoso the Parvenu said, "I defy him. It gabbles like I know not what —
believe it, the fellow's a shrewd fellow at a pink."

A "pink" is a stab. Benazzi was a discharged soldier, and as a soldier he had
experience in battle and so was dangerous. He was also an outlaw by necessity,
which meant that he was forced to do violence in order to survive.

Benazzi the Outlaw now criticized the commonwealth of beasts:

"If you don't believe me when I say that the commonwealth of beasts is
most politicly ordered, look:

"The lion roars, and the spaniel fawns — down, cur!"

The lion is dangerous and roars, but it is the fawning cocker spaniel that is
told, "Down, cur!"

Benazzi continued:

"The badger bribes the unicorn so that a jury may not pass judgment upon
his pillage."

Because of his use of bribery, the badger can avoid being punished for his
crime.

Benazzi continued:

"Here the bear fees the wolf, for he will not howl gratis — beasts call
pleading howling."

The bear pays the wolf money to plead for the bear in a court of law —
wolves will not do such pleading (as an attorney) for free.

Benazzi continued:

"So, then! There the horse complains of the ape's rank — very bad —
riding; the jockey makes faces, but is fined for it."

In this context, at this time, and in this society, the "jockey" is a
horse-dealer — the person who owns the horse. Although it is the ape that does
the rank — very wild — riding, it is the horse's owner who gets fined.

Benazzi continued:

"The stag is not jeered at by the monkey on account of its horns.

"The ass is not jeered at by the hare on account of its burden.

"The ox is not jeered at by the leopard on account of its yoke.

"Nor is the goat jeered at by the ram on account of its beard."

So far, so good — but it will not last.

Benazzi continued:

"Only the fox wraps itself warm in beaver, orders the cat to hunt mice, orders the elephant to toil, and orders the boar to gather acorns.

"All the while the fox grins, eats and grows fat, tells tales, laughs at everyone else, and sleeps safely at the lion's feet."

The other animals don't jeer at each other, but only the fox, which does not treat other animals well, lives a luxurious life without working for it, in part because the fox enjoys the protection of the lion.

The unicorn, which was bribed, and the lion, which protects the fox, are symbols of the United Kingdom and appear in the royal coat of arms.

Benazzi the Outlaw continued:

"Save ye, people."

This can mean 1) "Save yourselves, people," and/or 2) "May God save you, people."

Fulgoso the Parvenu said, "Why, save thee, too, if thou are of heaven's making. Who are you?"

He then said to Guzman, "Fear nothing, Don. We have our blades, we are metal-men ourselves, so let anyone who dares to, test us."

Guzman the Spaniard said to Benazzi the Outlaw, "Our brother speaks our mind — think whatever you please about it."

Benazzi the Outlaw said, "A match!"

The match could be a contest: 1) a fight between him and the other two, or 2) a lie-telling contest between him and the other two — Fulgoso and Guzman could have started the contest by pretending not to be afraid of Benazzi.

Benazzi said, "Observe well this switch that I am using as a riding-crop. With only this switch, I have dashed out the brains of thirteen Turks to the dozen for a breakfast."

He claimed that as a soldier, he had done good work to earn his breakfast: He had killed not a dozen Turks but a baker's dozen.

Fulgoso the Parvenu said, "What, man, thirteen! Is it possible that thou are not lying?"

Benazzi said, "I was once a scholar, but then I begged without receiving pity."

Many scholars are poor and need to be fed by others so that they can devote time to study, but no one gave him food.

Benazzi continued:

"From thence I practiced law, but there a scruple of conscience popped me over the bar — I was expelled from the society of lawyers because of my conscience.

"I turned soldier for a while, but I could not procure the letter of recommendation that would get me a promotion.

"I wanted to be a merchant, but a glut of land-rats gnawed me to the bones.

"I would have bought an official position, but the places were already filled and other people had guarantees to get the official positions when they became open.

"I attempted to pass into the court, but I lacked the credit to get the necessary clothes.

"Lastly, because of my good physique, I was forced into the galley-ships to row. I was taken prisoner, redeemed among other slaves by your lively-looking great man — they call him Auria — and I am now I know not who, where, or what.

"How do you like me now? Tell me."

Fulgoso the Parvenu said, "Thou are a fellow of all trades! What course of life do thou mean to follow next, huh? Tell me."

Guzman the Spaniard said, "Nor should thou be daunted, fellow; we ourselves have felt the frowns of fortune in our days."

Benazzi the Outlaw said, "I am extremely, exceedingly, hideously needy."

He especially needed food.

Levidolce, who had witnessed the entire scene from an upper window, threw down a bag of money and said, "Take that, enjoy it freely, wisely use it to the advantage of thy fate, and know the giver."

She wanted Benazzi the Outlaw to know who had given him the money.

She disappeared without giving anyone the time to see her and know who had thrown down the bag of money.

Fulgoso the Parvenu said, "Hey! A bag of money, indeed! Who dropped it?"

Looking around and seeing no one, he said, "Um, have we gypsies here?"

Gypsies were known for thievery.

In case a gypsy had decided to play Robin Hood with his money, Fulgoso checked to see if he still had it and said, "Oh, my money is safe."

He asked, "Was it your money, brother Don?"

Guzman the Spaniard said, "It wasn't mine. I seldom wear such unfashionable trash about me."

Moneybags, which were called purses, were tied to a person under the person's clothing.

The badly dressed Guzman, of course, gave the appearance of having little or no money.

Fulgoso the Parvenu asked Benazzi, "Has the purse any money in it, honest blade? A bots on empty purses!"

Bots are parasitic worms.

Guzman the Spaniard said, "We defy them."

Benazzi ordered, "Stand away from me, as you are mortal! You are dull, clod-headed lumps of mire and garbage. This is the land of fairies.

"Imperial queen of elves, I crouch to thee, vow my services, my blood, and my muscles to thee, sweet sovereign of largess and liberality."

Thinking of the money in the purse, he began to think about countries and the things for which they were most famous:

"A French tailor — neat!

"A Persian cook — dainty!

"Greek wines — rich!

"Flanders mares — stately!

"Spanish salads — poignant!

"Venetian whores — ravishing!

"English pimps — unmatchable!"

He then said, "Sirs, I am outfitted with what I need — I have money now and can buy food."

Fulgoso the Parvenu said about the queen of fairies, "All these are thy followers? Miserable pygmies!"

He added, "Prate sense, and don't be insane. I like thy disposition: It is pretty, it is odd, and so as one might say, I don't greatly mind if I give thee a job.

"Do thou want a master? If thou do, I'm for thee: I'll give you a job.

"Choose not to work for me, and I say, 'Go hang thee!'

"Bah, I scorn to back off, man."

Guzman the Spaniard advised Benazzi, "Don't forsake fair advancement; money, for certain, will quickly leave thee, like a friend who has cheated thee.

"Whoever holds money, holds a slippery eel by the tail. He loses it unless he grips it fast. Follow my advice."

"Excellent!" Benazzi said. "To what position shall I be admitted? Will I take care of the bedchamber, wardrobe, wine cellar, or stable?"

Fulgoso the Parvenu replied, "Why, one and all of them. Thou are welcome; let's shake hands on it."

They shook hands.

Fulgoso asked, "What is thy name?"

Benazzi the Outlaw said, "Parado, sir."

The word "parado" means parade ground.

Fulgoso the Parvenu said, "The great affairs I shall employ thee most in will be the gathering of gossip and news, and telling me what o'clock it is, as far as anything I know yet."

Benazzi/Parado said, "It is, sir, to speak punctually, some hour and half, eight three thirds of two seconds of one minute over at most, sir."

Fulgoso the Parvenu replied, "I do not ask thee the time now; or if I did, we are not much the wiser; and as for news —"

Benazzi/Parado stated the most important recent news: "Auria the fortunate is this day to be received with great solemnity at the city council-house; the streets are already thronged with lookers-on."

Fulgoso the Parvenu replied, "That's well remembered."

He then said, "Brother Don, let's trudge there now, or we shall arrive too late."

Guzman the Spaniard said, "By no means, brother."

He meant that they would by no means arrive late.

Fulgoso the Parvenu said to Benazzi/Parado, "Wait close, my ragged newcomer."

That meant: Stay close in case I need some service.

Benazzi/Parado replied, "I will stay as close to you as your shadows."

They exited.

— 3.2 —

Auria, Lord Adurni, Martino, Trelcatio, Aurelio, Piero, and Futelli talked together in a hall in Auria's house.

Auria said, "Your favors, with these honors, speak your bounties. And though the low deserts of my success appear in your interpretations of events fair and goodly, yet I attribute to a noble cause, and not to my abilities, the thanks due to them."

Auria was being honored for his excellent service in fighting the Turks, but he was humble. Rather than giving credit for his success to his own abilities, he was giving credit for the good cause for which he had fought.

He continued, "The Duke of Florence has too highly prized my duty in my service, by example, rather to cherish and encourage virtue in spirits of action than to crown the results of feeble undertakings."

He believed that the Duke of Florence had praised his — Auria's — efforts more than they deserved as a way of encouraging others to valiantly serve the state.

He continued, "As long as my life can stand in use, I shall no longer value it except as it stirs to pay that debt I owe my country for my birth and fortunes."

He wished to devote his life to serve his country.

Martino said, "Which to make good, our state of Genoa, not willing that a native of Genoa's own, so able for her safety, should take pension from any other prince, has cast upon you the government of Corsica."

Corsica is an island in the Mediterranean Sea, directly south of Genoa. Genoese ships stationed there served as a buffer for Genoa against the Turkish pirate ships.

Auria was being richly rewarded with power for his success as a military leader: He was very important to ensuring the safety of Genoa and places in which it had interests. Along with the power it gave Auria, Genoa would give much money.

Trelcatio, Auria's uncle, said, "Added thereto, besides the allowance yearly due, forever to you and to your heirs, the full revenue belonging to Savona, with the office of Admiral of Genoa."

Savona is a city close to Genoa.

Auria would govern Corsica, serve as the Admiral of Genoa, receive a yearly allowance, and get additional money from Savona.

As Admiral of Genoa, Auria would be protecting Genoa, Savona, and Corsica from the Turks. He would also be protecting other Italian cities.

Lord Adurni said, "Presenting by my hands from their public treasury a thousand ducats."

Whose public treasury? Apparently, the treasury of Genoa, which would perhaps include money from Savona and Corsica and perhaps other places.

Martino said, "But they set a limit of only one month of stay for your departure: no more."

Auria was required to leave for Corsica within a month.

Futelli said, "In all your great endeavors, may you grow thrifty, secure, and prosperous!"

Piero said, "If you please to rank among the humblest one who shall follow instructions under your command, I am ready to await the command."

He was willing to move to Corsica and serve under Auria.

Auria said, "Oh, still the state engages me as her creature, with the burden unequal for my weakness."

Still humble, Auria was saying that the state was building him very high — higher than he deserved.

Auria said to the others present, "To you, gentlemen, I will prove to be friendly and honest, and mindful of all."

Lord Adurni said to Auria, "In memory, my Lord — such is your title now — of your late fortunate exploits, the council, among their general acts, have registered the Great Duke of Florence's letters, witness of your merit, to stand in characters upon record."

Lord Auria said, "Load upon load!"

He was being laden with honors.

He continued, "Let not my lack of modesty" — he did not lack modesty — "trespass against good manners. I must devote myself to being alone in order to compose this weighty business and moderately digest so large a plenty, for fear it may swell into an excess that will make me ill."

Lord Auria needed time to be alone to take in his honors: He feared being made excessively proud by them.

"May I be bold to press a visit?" Lord Adurni asked.

"At your pleasure," Lord Auria replied.

He did not mean a visit at this moment, but later.

Lord Auria then said to all present, "Good time of day, and peace!"

All present replied, "Health to your lordship!"

Everyone except Lord Adurni and Futelli exited.

Lord Adurni asked, "Is there any news about Spinella yet?"

She had disappeared.

Futelli said, "Her track is quite lost; our 'hounds' can find no footprints, and none of our 'hounds' give tongue — howl — as they would if they found her track.

"However matters are huddled up, I fear, my lord, that her husband carries little peace about him."

Lord Adurni's possible attempted seduction of Spinella had been hushed up, or people had at least attempted to hush it up, but no doubt Lord Auria had learned about it and it would worry and/or anger him even if he showed a calm face in public.

Lord Adurni said, "Let danger fall where danger can; Spinella is a goodness above temptation; she is more to be adored than tested and examined. I'm to blame, I am sure."

Futelli said, "Levidolce, for her part, too, laughed at Malfato's frenzy — that is just how she termed it.

"But as for you, my lord, Levidolce said she thanked your charity, which lent her crooked soul, before it left her body, some respite, wherein it might learn again the means of growing straight."

Levidolce had told her great-uncle, Martino, that she wanted to repent her sins; here was additional evidence that she was sincere in her desire to repent.

Lord Adurni said, "She has found mercy, which I will seek and sue for."

Such mercy comes from God.

Futelli said, "You are fortunate."

Lord Adurni wanted to do the right thing.

In another room in Lord Auria's house, Auria and Aurelio talked together.

Lord Auria listed his new honors: "Count of Savona! Genoa's admiral! Lord-governor of Corsica! Designated and enrolled as a worthy dignitary of my country! Sought and petitioned-to, praised, courted, flattered!"

He added, "Surely, this body of mine grows in size because of these honors! A tympany — a tumor — of greatness puffs up my narrow chest too monstrously."

He said to Aurelio, "How surely thou do view with malice these extremes, uncomforting man!"

The "extremes" were extreme honors.

Lord Auria continued, "When I was needy and cast naked on the flats of barren pity, abated to an ebb so low that boys riding hobby-horses frisked about me without plunging to the ground and so without falling as low as I was then, you could chat gravely then in formal tones, and reason most paradoxically. Now contempt and willful grudge at my uprising becalms your learned noise."

Previously, before Lord Auria's present success, Aurelio had been able to talk gravely and reason paradoxically in his presence. "Reason paradoxically" perhaps means to talk to and treat with respect a man whose status is low.

Now, however, Lord Auria thought that because of his success Aurelio no longer talked and reasoned that way. According to Lord Auria, Aurelio spoke to him with contempt and willful grudge.

Aurelio had told Lord Auria about finding Spinella and Lord Adurni alone together in a private chamber.

Aurelio said, "Such flourish, Auria, flies with so swift a gale that it will waft thy sudden joys into a faithless harbor."

A flourish is a fanfare that announces the arrival of a VIP. In this case, Lord Adurni was being brought into their conversation. If Lord Adurni had slept with Lord Auria's wife, it certainly would reduce the intensity of Lord Auria's joys.

Lord Auria asked, "Can thou mutter evil?"

He continued, "I observed your dullness and sluggishness while the whole gang crowed to me. Listen! My triumphs are echoing under every roof; the air is narrowed by the sound, there is not room enough for all of the triumphant sounds to turn in, but not a single triumphal thought pierces into the grief that cabins here in my chest."

At this time, one meaning of "to narrow" was "to oppress."

He continued, "Here, through a creek, a little inlet, crawls a fiery flake no bigger than a sister's thread. The fiery flake sets the region of my heart on fire."

The Fates were three mythological sisters who commanded the pulse of life; they controlled human life. Clotho spun the thread of life. Lachesis measured the thread of life, determining how long a person lived. Atropos cut the thread of life; when the thread was cut, the person died.

Right now, it felt to Lord Auria as if his thread of life was burning.

Lord Auria continued, "I had a kingdom once, but I am deposed from all that royalty of blessed content by a confederacy between love and frailty."

His kingdom had been his happy marriage, but "a confederacy between love and frailty" was making him unhappy.

The love could be that of Spinella and the frailty could be that of her supposed infidelity.

Or the love could be the friendship of Aurelio and the frailty could be Aurelio's need to tell Lord Auria of Spinella's supposed infidelity.

Aurelio replied, "Glories in public view only add to misery, which travails in unrest at home."

The unrest at Lord Auria's home was due to Spinella's supposed infidelity. Being publicly acclaimed while being privately unhappy can lead to further unhappiness: One can feel worse because one knows he or she should be enjoying the public acclaim.

Lord Auria said, "At home! That home Aurelio speaks of I have lost, and, which is worse, even after I have rolled about, toiled like a pilgrim round this globe of earth, wearied with care and overworn with age, and when I am lodged in the grave, I am still not yet at home.

"There in the grave rots only half of me, the other part — my wife — sleeps Heaven knows where.

"I wish that she and I — my wife, I mean — but why, alas, do I talk about my wife? I should talk, perhaps, about 'the woman.'"

In marriage, two become one, but Lord Auria and Spinella were now separated.

He continued, "I wish that we had together fed on any thrown-away coarse and moldy parings of food rather than lived divided like this! I could have begged for both of us, for it would be a pity if she should ever have felt so much extremity of hunger."

Aurelio said, "Patience is not required in wrongs of such vile nature. You pity her. Think rather about getting revenge!"

Lord Auria said, "Revenge! For what, uncharitable friend? On whom? Let's speak a little, please, with reason.

"You found Spinella in Lord Adurni's house. It is likely he gave her welcome — very likely. Her sister and another person were with her — so!"

The other person was Amoretta.

Lord Auria continued, "She and they were invited, and that was nobly done; but Lord Adurni was with Spinella privately chambered.

"A man deserves no wife of worthy quality who does not dare to trust her virtue in the tests of any danger."

Aurelio said, "But I broke open the doors upon them."

Lord Auria replied, "Indeed, you did, and it was a slovenly, low, and lewd presumption and it was punishable by a sharp rebuke.

"I tell you, sir, that I in my younger years have by the stealth of privacy enjoyed being in a lady's private chambers, where to have profaned that shrine of chastity and innocence with one unhallowed word would have exiled the freedom of such favor into scorn."

As a young man, Lord Auria himself had been alone with a lady in her private rooms, and he had behaved like a perfect gentleman and had not attempted a seduction.

Lord Auria continued, "Had any man alive then ventured there with a foul interpretation of what was happening, I would have stamped the justice of my unguilty and innocent truth upon his heart."

He would have fought any man who had forced open the door because the man suspected immoral behavior was occurring there.

The motto of the Order of the Garter is "*Honi soit qui mal y pense*," which means, "Shame on him who thinks this is evil."

King Edward III was dancing with Joan of Kent, his daughter-in-law, when her garter slipped down her leg. Other guests saw this and sniggered, and Edward III said the words that became the motto of the Order of the Garter.

Aurelio said, "Lord Adurni might have done as you did and behaved like a perfect gentleman, but he blushed: The conscience of his fault in coward blood blushed at the quick surprise of my forcing open the door."

The blush could have been due to guilt, but people turn red for other reasons, including anger. Another reason could be being embarrassed for the man who had so badly misinterpreted what was actually happening.

Lord Auria said, "Oh, bah, bah! How badly some argue in their sour reproof against a party liable to law!"

Lord Auria now argued that if Lord Adurni had been guilty of seduction, he would have behaved differently: "For had that lord offended with that creature, her presence would have doubled every strength of man in him, and justified the forfeit of noble shame."

In other words, if he were actually guilty of seduction or attempted seduction, the presence of the woman would have caused him to brazen out the situation and not feel shame.

Lord Auria continued, "But if they were innocent, it would be enough for both of them to correct your rudeness with a smile only."

The smile would probably be of scorn and contempt.

Aurelio said, "It is well that you make such use of neighbors' courtesy. Some kinds of beasts are tame and meek, and hug their injuries and keep them to themselves. Such behavior leads to a reputation, too!"

Lord Auria said, "Don't use uncivil language, although you feel violent emotion, friend."

Aurelio asked, "For what reason, then, do you think she is absenting herself if she is blameless? You grant, of course, that your triumphs are proclaimed, and I personally told her about your return. Where is she lying hidden all this time?"

Lord Auria said, "The reason for her absence rests in you.

"Now I come to thee. We have exchanged private thoughts, Aurelio, from our years of childhood. Let me acknowledge with what pride I regard a man who is so faithful and honest as my fast friend.

"Thou are the friend who, if I speak fully, has never failed, by teaching trust to me, to learn of mine. I wished myself thine equal; if I aimed to commit a wrong, it was in an envy of thy goodness.

"So dearly — witness with me my integrity — I laid thee up to heart, that from my love for thee my love for my wife was but distinguished in her sex.

"Give back and restore to me that holy signature — that holy distinguishing mark — of friendship, which has been cancelled, defaced, and plucked off by this action of yours regarding my wife, or I shall settle up our accounts, scored on the tally of my vengeance, without all former compliments."

In other words, either restore to me the friendship that you have violated, or I shall take revenge against you for your action. In taking revenge, I shall not take into account our former friendship.

Aurelio said, "Do you imagine I fawn upon your fortunes, or intrude in your life upon the hope of bettering my estate? Is that why you would cashier me at a minute's warning?

"No, Auria, I dare vie with your respects. Put my respects and your respects into the balance, and the two scales shall weigh the same.

"Perhaps the offer, so frankly vowed at your departure first of settling me a partner in your purchase leads you into an opinion of some ends of mercenary falsehood; yet such wrong least suits a noble soul."

Aurelio was accusing Lord Auria of thinking that he, Aurelio, was telling lies against Spinella because Lord Auria had said that he would make Aurelio his heir. If Lord Auria were to stay married to Spinella and have children with her, their children would be Lord Auria's heirs. Aurelio would not inherit Lord Auria's wealth.

Lord Auria said, "By all my sorrows, what you accuse me of thinking is too coarse."

Aurelio said, "Since, then, the occasion presents the discontinuance of our friendship, use your liberty and do whatever you like. As for my part, I am resolute to die the same as my life has professed me."

Lord Auria said, "Bah! Your faith was never in suspicion.

"But consider, neither the lord nor lady, nor the bawd that shuffled them together, whose name is Opportunity, have fastened stain on my unquestioned name.

"No, it was my friend's rash indiscretion that was the bellows that blew the coal, which is now kindled to a flame that will light my friend's slander to all wandering eyes."

The slander was that Spinella had been unfaithful to Lord Auria.

Auria continued, "Some men in giddy zeal overdo that office they catch at, of whose number is Aurelio."

The office was that of a friend. Aurelio had supposed that he had been looking out for the interests of his friend Lord Auria when he had burst into the private chamber in which were Spinella and Lord Adurni.

Lord Auria continued, "For I am certain — certain — that it would have been impossible, if you had stood wisely silent, for anything other than that my Spinella, trembling on her knee, would have accused her breach of truth and would have begged a speedy execution on her trespass."

What did he mean by "her breach of truth" and "her trespass"?

Would it be infidelity, or would it be being in a position in which infidelity could be falsely inferred?

Lord Auria continued, "Then with a justice as lawful as the magistrate's, I might have drawn my sword against Lord Adurni — my sword that now is sheathed and rusted in the scabbard. Good thanks to your cheap providence!"

He might have drawn his sword against Lord Adurni because Lord Adurni had made Spinella guilty of infidelity, or because he had put her in a position in which infidelity could be falsely inferred.

Lord Auria continued, "Once more I make demand — my wife — you — sir —"

He was so angry he could not speak.

He drew his sword.

Aurelio said, "Roar louder. The noise does not frighten me; threaten your enemies, and prove you're a valiant man with your tongue.

"Now must follow, by way of method, the exact condition of rage that runs to mutiny in friendship.

"Lord Auria, come on; this weapon does not look pale" — he drew his sword — "at the sight of your weapon.

"Again hear, and believe it, that what I have done was well done and well meant. Twenty times over, if I had the opportunity to do it again, I'd do it and do it, and I'd boast that the pains were religious and just and the right things to do.

"Yet since you shake me and my friendship off, I slightly value any other kind of severity."

Calming down, for he was almost always a calm and rational man, Lord Auria said, "May honor and duty stand as my witnesses that anger never did purpose the ungentle usage of my sword against Aurelio."

That anger did never purpose the ungentle usage of Lord Auria's sword against Aurelio does not rule out the possibility that anger did purpose the gentle use of Lord Auria's sword against Aurelio. The word "gentle" can mean "noble and honorable."

Lord Auria sheathed his sword, and then Aurelio sheathed his sword.

Lord Auria continued, "I wish that I would rather lack my hands — indeed, friend, let me rather lack a heart, than ever allow such folly to enter here in my breast."

This was not a lie.

He continued, "If I must lose Spinella, let me not proceed to misery by also losing my Aurelio. We, through madness, frame strange ideas in our wandering, incoherent brains, and prate about things as we pretend they were.

"Join your help to my efforts, good man, and let us listen to hear if we can learn anything about this straying soul that is Spinella, and until we find her, let us bear our discomfort quietly."

Aurelio said, "Doubtless, she may soon be discovered."

"That's spoken cheerfully," Lord Auria said. "Why, there's a friend now! Auria and Aurelio at odds! Oh, it cannot be — it must not, and it shall not —

"But look, Castanna's here!"

Castanna, Spinella's sister, walked over to them.

Lord Auria complimented her: "Welcome, fair figure of a choice jewel locked up in a cabinet because it is more precious than the public view should sully."

The most valuable jewels tend to be locked up securely; less valuable jewels are worn in public.

Castanna said, "Sir, how you are informed, or on what terms of prejudice, opinion sways your confidence against my course or custom, I don't know."

She was worried that Lord Auria was angry at her.

She continued, "Much anger, if my fears do not persuade falsely, sits on this gentleman's — Aurelio's — stern brow, yet, sir, if an unhappy maiden's word may find credit, as I wish harm to nobody on earth, so I wish that all good folks may wish no harm to me!"

Lord Auria said, "None does, sweet sister-in-law."

Castanna said, "If they do, may dear Heaven forgive them — that is my prayer. But perhaps you might conceive — and yet I think you should not — that I am at fault in my sister's absence.

"Indeed, it is nothing like it is said to be, nor was I knowing of any private speech my Lord Adurni intended to have with my sister, except for speech that was civil entertainment. Indeed, what hurt can occur because of conversation, if that conversation is modest?

"Surely, noblemen will show that they are such — noble — with those of their own rank — and that was all my sister can be charged with."

Lord Auria asked, "Isn't she, friend, an excellent maiden?"

Castanna was an unmarried maiden.

Aurelio replied, "She deserves the best of fortunes. I have always spoken of her as being virtuous."

He had earlier accused Castanna of consenting in the immoral activity of Spinella and Lord Adurni.

Castanna said, "With your leave, you used most cruel language to my sister, enough to frighten her wits. You were not very kind to me myself. She sighed when you had left, and she desired that no one should follow her. And, truly, I was so full of weeping, I did not notice well which way she went."

Lord Auria asked, "She didn't stay inside the house, then?"

He meant his and his wife's house.

Of course, Lord Auria had just arrived home.

Castanna said, "Alas, she did not — Aurelio was surpassingly rough."

"Strange!" Lord Auria said. "She is nowhere to be found?"

"Not yet," Castanna said, "but I swear on my life that before many hours pass, I shall hear from her."

"Shall thou?" Lord Auria said. "You are a worthy maiden. Thou have brought to my sick heart a medicinal cordial."

He said to Aurelio, "Friend, good news!"

He then said, "Most sweet Castanna!"

Aurelio said, "I hope that soon Castanna hears from Spinella!"

Benazzi stood alone on a street. He was using the name "Parado" now, and he was serving Fulgoso the Parvenu.

Benazzi/Parado said, "The paper that was in the purse thrown to me gave me directions. This is the place the paper appointed, and this is the time the paper appointed. Here I dance attendance and wait. Ah, here she is already."

Levidolce, Benazzi's divorced wife, walked over to him.

Benazzi still looked like an outlaw, but Levidolce was not wearing any kind of disguise.

"Parado!" Levidolce said. "I overheard your name."

Benazzi/Parado said, "I am a mushroom, sprung up in a minute by the sunshine of your benevolent grace."

A mushroom is someone who rises quickly in social status. Benazzi had been an outlaw, but the money Levidolce had thrown to him had relieved his distress considerably. In addition, he had found a job serving Fulgoso the Parvenu.

Benazzi/Parado continued, "Liberality and hospitable compassion, most magnificent beauty, have for a long time lain bedridden in the ashes of the old world until now. Your illustrious charity has raked up the dead embers, by giving life to a worm inevitably devoted to you, as you shall please to new-shape me."

Levidolce thought, *He is a grateful man, it seems. Where gratitude has harbor, a stock of other becoming accomplished qualities must necessarily inhabit the same place.*

She asked out loud, "What country claims your birth? What country are you from?"

"None," Benazzi/Parado replied. "I was born at sea, as my mother sailed from Cape Ludugory to Cape Cagliari, toward Africa, in Sardinia. I was raised in Aquilastro, and when I became a young man, I put myself in service under the Spanish Viceroy, until I was taken prisoner by the Turks.

"I have tasted in my days a handsome store of good and bad, and I am thankful for both."

Levidolce said, "You seem the child, then, of honest parents."

Benazzi/Parado said, "They were reputed to be no less than honest. Many children often inherit the lands of those who perhaps never begot them. My mother's husband was a very old man at my birth, but no man is too old to father his wife's child."

It is true that if a man grows old enough, that man will become biologically impotent. Nature cannot trust an old man to be around to raise a child. In the interests of peace, however, it can be a good idea to pretend that the old man is the biological father.

It is also true that a husband can be very old, yet father — that is, raise — his wife's child.

Benazzi/Parado continued, "I am sure I will always prove myself to be entirely your servant."

"Do you dare to be secret?" Levidolce asked.

"Yes," Benazzi/Parado replied.

"And do you dare to act quickly?" Levidolce asked.

"Yes," Benazzi/Parado replied.

"But also be sure of hand and sure of spirit?" Levidolce asked.

"Yes, yes," Benazzi/Parado replied.

"I will not use many words," Levidolce said. "The lack of time prevents their use, but a man of quality has robbed my honor."

"Robbed my honor" can mean "raped me," but it can also mean "seduced me."

"Name him," Benazzi/Parado said.

"Adurni," Levidolce replied.

"He shall bleed," Benazzi/Parado said.

Levidolce added, "Malfato scornfully rejected the love I offered to him."

Benazzi/Parado said, "Yoke them in death."

Apparently, he meant that he could kill both Lord Adurni and Malfato.

"Yoke them in death" has another, sexual meaning. One meaning of "to yoke" is to hug and couple. One meaning of "to die" is to have an orgasm.

Benazzi/Parado then asked, "What's my reward for doing this?"

"Propose it, and enjoy it," Levidolce said.

"I want you for my wife," Benazzi/Parado answered.

"Ha!" Levidolce exclaimed.

"Nothing else will do," Benazzi/Parado said. "Deny me, and I'll betray your counsels and cause your ruin. Your other choice is to do the feat courageously. Marry me or be ruined. Consider."

"I do," Levidolce said. "Dispatch the task I have imposed on you, and then claim what I have promised."

"That won't happen, pretty one," Benazzi/Parado said. "We'll marry first, or farewell."

He started to leave.

"Wait," Levidolce said. "Think about what I have confessed and know what a plague thou are drawing into thy bosom. Although I blush to say it, know that I have, without any sense of shame or honor, forsaken a lawful marriage bed in order to amuse myself between Lord Adurni's arms."

Benazzi/Parado said, "This lord's."

He was asking if Lord Adurni were the man of quality who had robbed her honor.

"He is the same," Levidolce said. "There is more. Not content with him, I courted a newer pleasure, but I was there refused by the man I named so recently."

"Malfato?" Benazzi/Parado asked.

"That is right," Levidolce said. "I am henceforth resolutely bent to print my follies on their hearts, and then I will change my life for some rare penance."

This is not the way repentance works. If you repent, you forgive now. You don't get revenge first and then repent.

Levidolce asked, "Can thou love me now?"

"I love you better," Benazzi/Parado said. "I do believe it is possible you may mend. All this breaks off no bargain."

"Accept my hand," Levidolce said. "With this hand comes a faith as constant as vows can urge; nor shall my haste prevent this contract, which only death must divorce."

They were now legally engaged to be married.

"Set the time for the wedding," Benazzi/Parado said.

"Meet here tomorrow night," Levidolce said. "We will make further decisions, as is suitable for us."

Benazzi/Parado asked, "What is the name of my new love?"

He had recognized her, but he did not want her to know who he was.

"Levidolce," she answered. "Be confident I bring a worthy dowry to you. But you'll flee."

"Not I, by all that's noble!" Benazzi/Parado said. "Give me a kiss."

She kissed him.

As he exited, he said, "Farewell, dear fate!"

Alone, Levidolce said, "Love is sharp-sighted and can pierce through the cunning of disguises."

In other words, she had recognized him.

Because she was not wearing a disguise, he must have recognized her. She had to know that.

Levidolce added, "False pleasures, I cashier you — I dismiss you. Fair truth, welcome!"

"False pleasures" can include the pleasures of adultery. "Fair truth" can include faithfulness in marriage.

CHAPTER 4
— 4.1 —

Malfato and Spinella spoke together in a room in Malfato's house. Malfato and Spinella were first cousins.

"You are safe here, my sad cousin," Malfato said. "If you please, you may repeat the circumstances of what you recently discoursed. My ears are gladly open, for I myself am in such hearty league with solitary thoughts that pensive language charms my attention."

Spinella said, "But by how much more in him my husband's honors sparkle clearly, by so much more they tempt belief to credit the wreck and ruin of my injured name."

When a man rises high, such as Lord Auria recently had, some people are tempted to pull him back down again. In Lord Auria's case, they could do that by believing the gossip that was now being told about his wife, Spinella herself.

Malfato said, "Why, cousin, even if the earth would cleave to the roots of trees as they fell, the seas and heavens be mingled in disorder, your purity with unfrightened eyes might look intently at the uproar. It is the guilty who tremble at horrors, not the innocent. You're cruel in censuring a liberty that is allowed."

Which liberty? Gossip, which is free speech? Certainly, Malfato believed that Spinella's good character would triumph over any malicious gossip told about her.

He continued, "Speak freely, gentle cousin. Was Lord Adurni importunately wanton?"

Spinella said, "He was in excess of entertainment; otherwise, he was not importunately wanton."

Was she being deliberately kind in interpreting what had happened? Can an attempted seduction be regarded as a social invitation to an entertainment?

Malfato asked, "Not the boldness of an uncivil courtship?"

"What that meant I never understood," Spinella said.

Sometimes, women pretend not to know things that they really know. They know these things privately, but pretend not to know them in their public life. Pretending ignorance is a way to maintain innocence.

She continued, "I have at once set bars between my best of earthly joys and the best of men — he is as excellent a man as lives without comparison; his love to me was matchless."

The bars were between herself, and her husband: between her enjoyment of her husband, and her husband. She had separated herself from her husband.

Malfato said, "Yet, suppose, sweet cousin, that I could name a creature whose affection followed your Lord Auria in the height; affection to you, even to Spinella, affection as true and settled as ever Lord Auria's was, can, is, or will be. You may not chide the story."

Spinella said, "Fortune's favorites are flattered, but the miserable are not flattered."

Malfato now began to tell Spinella that he loved her:

"Listen to a strange tale, which thus the author sighed. A kinsman of Spinella — so it runs — her father's sister's son, some time before Auria the fortunate possessed her beauties, became enamored of such rare perfections as she was stored with.

"He fed his idle hopes with the possibilities of lawful conquest.

"He proposed — carefully considered — each difficulty in pursuit of what his vain supposal styled his own.

"He found in the argument only one flaw of conscience, which was the nearness of their bloods — they were first cousins. This was an unhappy scruple, but easily dispensed with, had any friend's advice resolved the doubt."

The word "doubt" can also mean "fear." The friend could have disposed of the doubt and fear with his or her advice.

Malfato continued, "Still on he loved and loved, and wished and wished.

"Sometimes he began to speak, yet soon broke off, and still the fondling dared not — because he dared not."

Spinella said, "It was wonderful."

Malfato said, "Exceedingly wonderful, beyond all wonder, yet it is known for truth after her marriage, when nothing remained of expectation to such fruitless dotage.

"His reason then — now — then — could not reduce the violence of passion, although he vowed never to unlock that secret, and scarcely to her, Spinella herself; and in addition he resolved not to come near her presence, but to avoid all opportunities, however presented to him."

Spinella said, "An understanding dulled by the infelicity of constant sorrow finds it difficult to take in and understand pregnant novelty and important news. My ears receive the words you utter, cousin, but my thoughts are fastened on another subject."

Malfato said, "Can you embrace your own woes and make them so like a darling, and play the tyrant with a partner in them?"

Malfato was suffering from unrequited love, but Spinella was showing no pity to him.

He continued, "Then I am thankful for this opportunity: Urged by fatal and enjoined necessity to stand up in defense of injured virtue, I will against anyone — I except no one, including no person of quality and high rank — maintain all these suppositions about you to be misapplied, dishonest, false, and villainous."

Spinella began, "Dear cousin, as you're a gentleman —"

Malfato interrupted, "— I'll bless that hand whose honorable pity seals the passport for my incessant turmoils to their rest."

He was thinking of fighting a duel to defend her honor. Dying in the duel meant that his unhappiness would cease.

He continued, "If I prevail — which heaven forbid! — these ages that shall inherit ours may tell posterity that Spinella had Malfato for a kinsman. Future ages will be made jealous of her fame because of his noble love."

"No more," Spinella said. "I dare not hear it."

"All is said," Malfato said. "Henceforth a syllable shall never proceed from my unpleasant and unwelcome voice of amorous folly —"

The entrance of Castanna interrupted him.

Castanna said, "Your summons told me to come here; I have come.

"Sister, my sister, it was an unkind action not to take me along with thee."

"Chide her for it," Malfato said. "Castanna, this house is as freely yours as your father's ever was."

Castanna said, "We believe it to be so, although your recent strange aloofness had made us wonder —

"But for what reason, sister, do thou keep your silence and distance? Am I not welcome to thee?"

Spinella asked, "Is Auria safe and sound?

"Oh, please do not hear me call him 'husband' before thou can resolve what kind of wife his fury terms me, the runaway. Speak quickly. Yet do not — stop, Castanna — I am lost! His friend Aurelio has told him that I am a bad woman, and he, the good man, believes it."

Castanna began, "Now, in truth —"

"Stop!" Spinella said. "My heart trembles — I perceive thy tongue is pregnant with ills, and hastens to tell those ill tidings.

"I would not treat Castanna so.

"First tell me, shortly and truly tell me, how he is."

"He is in perfect health," Castanna said.

"For that I give my thanks to Heaven," Spinella said.

Malfato said to himself, "The world has not another wife like this."

He then said to Spinella, "Cousin, you will not hear your sister speak, so much your strong emotion rules you."

Spinella said, "I will listen now to what she pleases to tell me.

"Go on, Castanna."

Castanna said, "Your most noble husband is deaf to all reports about you, and only grieves at the causeless absence of his soul's love: Spinella."

Malfato said to Spinella, "Why, see, cousin, now! This is good news!"

Spinella said, "It is good news indeed!"

Castanna said, "He will value no counsel and advice, he takes no pleasure in his greatness, he admits of no likelihood at all that you are living; if you were living, he's certain that it would be impossible you could conceal your welcomes to him, because you are all one with him.

"But as for jealousy, suspicion, or mistrust concerning your dishonor, he both laughs at and scorns it."

Spinella asked, "Does he?"

Lord Auria truly scorned such gossip about her.

Malfato said, "Therein Auria shows himself to deserve his happiness."

Castanna said, "I think this news should cause some reaction in you, sister — you are not well."

Spinella was quiet.

"Not well!" Malfato said.

Spinella said, "I am unworthy —"

Malfato asked, "Of whom? What? Why?"

Spinella said to Malfato, "Go, cousin."

She said to her sister, "Come, Castanna."

Malfato exited in one direction; Spinella and Castanna exited in another direction.

Trelcatio, Piero, and Futelli spoke together in an apartment in Trelcatio's house. Trelcatio was Lord Auria's uncle.

Trelcatio said, "Members of the council are already sitting: I will arrive late. Now, therefore, gentlemen, this house is free for you to use. As your intentions are sober, your pains shall be accepted."

Futelli replied, "Mirth sometimes falls into earnest, signor."

"We, for our parts, aim at the best," Piero said.

They were playing a practical joke on Amoretta, old Trelcatio's daughter, by having two foolish men court her and by telling her that the two foolish men were highly born.

Some people might think that the practical joke was cruel, but Trelcatio believed that the intentions of Futelli and Piero were basically good.

Trelcatio replied, "If you two are not aiming for the best, then you wrong yourselves and me. May you have good success!"

He exited to go to the council.

Piero said, "Futelli, it is our wisest course to follow our pastime with discretion, by which means we may ingratiate, as our business hits, our undertakings to great Auria's favor."

Lord Auria and Amoretta were cousins, and if Futelli and Piero were to help Amoretta get over her obsession with the highly born and the number of horses that pulled their coaches, they would help both her and by extension Lord Auria, who naturally would want his cousin to be a good person. By helping Lord Auria, Futelli and Piero could very well help themselves.

Futelli said, "I grow quite weary of this lazy custom, attending on the fruitless hopes of service for food and ragged clothing.

"A wit? That would be a shrewd preferment! Study some scurrilous jests, grow old, and beg!

"No, let them who love foul linen be admired. I'll run a new course."

He had been serving Lord Adurni, but he saw little hope of rising in society if he continued to do that. He wanted to find another way to rise in society.

Piero said, "Get the coin we spend. And knock on the head those who jeer our earnings."

Music began to sound. It was a gift to Amoretta from one of her suitors.

Futelli said, "Hush, man! One suitor is coming."

Piero said, "The other suitor follows."

Futelli said, "Don't be so loud."

He saw Amoretta and said, "Here comes Madonna Sweet-lips."

He then imitated her lisp: "Mithtreth, in thooth, forthooth, will lithp it to uth."

Amoretta's lisp turned S's into Th's, and G's into D's, and sometimes R's into W's or other sounds.

Amoretta walked over to them and said, "Dentlemen, then ye."

She meant, "Gentlemen, den ye."

In this society, this meant: "Gentlemen, good evening!"

She continued, "Ith thith muthic yourth, or can you tell what great man'th fiddleth made it?

"Tith vedee pretty noyth, but who thould thend it?"

Piero asked, "Don't you yourself know, lady?"

Amoretta answered, "I do not uthe to [use to — that is, usually] thpend lip-labor upon quethtionths that I mythelf can anthwer."

"No, sweet madam," Futelli said. "Your lips are destined to a better use, or else the proverb fails of lisping maids."

This is the proverb: "None kitheth like the lithping lass."

Amoretta, who knew the proverb, said, "Kithing you mean; pway, come behind with your mockths, then. My lipths will therve the one to kith the other."

Amoretta knew that Futelli was mocking her lisp; she didn't let it worry her, but she did say that her lips would kiss each other.

She asked, "Now, whath neckth?"

Some singers sang these lyrics:

"*What ho! We come to be merry!*

"*Open the doors! A jovial crew,*

"*Lusty boys and free, and very,*

"*Very, very lusty boys are we!*

"*We can drink till all look blue,*

"*Dance, sing, and roar.*

"*Never give o'er*

"*As long as we have ever an eye to see.*"

The next part of the song included lisping:

"*Pithee, pithee, leth's come in.*

"*One thall all oua favours win.*

"*Dently, dently, we thall pass;*

"*None kitheth like the lithping lass.*"

Piero said, "What! Do you call this a song?"

Amoretta answered, "Yeth, a delithious thing, and wondroth pretty."

Futelli thought, *A very country-catch!*

A country-catch is a rustic song, but Futelli was also referring to Amoretta. He may have thought of her as a "cunt-try [to] catch."

Futelli said, "Doubtless some prince most likely has sent it to celebrate your night's repose."

Amoretta said, "Think ye tho, thignor? It muth be, then, thome unknown obthcure pwinth who thuns the light."

Piero said, "Perhaps he is the Prince of Darkness."

The Prince of Darkness is the Devil.

"Of darkneth!" Amoretta said. "Who ith he?"

Futelli said, "A matchless courtier: He woos and wins more beauties to his love than all the kings on earth."

Amoretta asked, "Whea thandeth hith court, pway?"

Futelli said, "This gentleman who is approaching, I presume, has more relation to his court than I do, and comes in time to inform you about it."

Fulgoso the Parvenu walked over to them.

Amoretta said, "Think you tho? I'm thure you know him."

Piero said, "Lady, you'll perceive that it is so."

Yes, the Prince of Darkness probably knew something about the activities of both Futelli and Piero.

Fulgoso the Parvenu thought, *She seems in my first entrance to admire me. I declare that she eyes me all over. Fulg, she's thine own!*

Piero said, "Noble Fulgoso."

Fulgoso the Parvenu said, "Did you hear the music? It was I who brought it. Wasn't it tickling? Ah, ha!"

Amoretta asked, "Pway, what pwinth thent it?"

She thought that Fulgoso was the man-servant of a prince who had sent the music.

Using the majestic plural, Fulgoso the Parvenu said, "Prince! No prince, but we. We set the ditty and composed the song. There's not a note of music or foot of verse in it but our own and the pure trodden mortar of this brain. We can do things and things."

The mortar of his brain cemented the music and words together. The mortar of his brain can be described as completely trodden.

Amoretta said, "Dood! Thing it youa thelf, then."

"No, no," Fulgoso the Parvenu said. "I could never sing more than a tomcat or even an owlet. But you shall hear me whistle it."

He whistled.

Amoretta said, "Thith thing'th thome jethter. Thurely he belongth to the Pwinth of Darkneth."

Piero said, "Yes, and I'll tell you what his office is. His prince delights himself exceedingly in birds of diverse kinds; this gentleman is the keeper and instructor of his blackbirds. He learned his skill first from his father's wagon-driver."

Amoretta said, "It ith wonderful to thee by what thrange means thome men are raised to plathes."

Fulgoso the Parvenu said, "I do hear you, and I thank you heartily for your good wills in setting forth my abilities, but what I live on is simple trade of money from my lands.

"Hang spongers and parasites! I am no cheater or trickster!"

Amoretta asked, "Ith it pothible?"

Guzman the Spaniard walked over to them.

Amoretta asked, "Bleth uth. Who'th thith?"

"Oh, it is the man of might," Futelli said.

Guzman the Spaniard said, "May my address to beauty lay no scandal upon my martial honor, since even Mars, whom, as in war, in love I imitate, could not resist the shafts of Cupid; therefore, as with the god of war, I deign to stoop."

"To deign" is "to condescend." He was condescending to stoop and court Amoretta.

He continued, "Lady, grant, Love's goddess like, to yield your fairer hand to these lips, the portals of valiant breath that has overturned an army."

He did well to compare Amoretta to Love's goddess: Venus. His breath, however, had a quality in addition to valiant: His breath was bad.

Amoretta said, "May faya weather protect me! What a thorm ith thith?"

Futelli said to Guzman, "Oh, Don, keep off at a further distance — yet a little further; don't you see how your strong breath has terrified the lady?"

Guzman the Spaniard said, "I'll stop the breath of war, and breathe as gently as a perfumed pair of sucking bellows in some sweet lady's chamber, for I can speak lion-like or sheep-like, when I please."

Futelli said, "Stand by, then, without noise, for a while, brave Don, and let her only view your body parts; they'll take her."

To "take" a woman can mean to have sex with her.

"I'll publish them in silence," Guzman the Spaniard said.

Piero said, "Stand over there, Fulgoso the magnificent."

"Here?" Fulgoso the Parvenu asked.

"Just there," Piero said. "Let her survey you both. You'll be her choice — never doubt it, man."

"I cannot doubt it, man," Fulgoso the Parvenu replied.

"But don't speak until I tell you," Piero said.

"May I whistle?" Fulgoso the Parvenu asked.

"A little to yourself, to pass the time," Piero said.

Amoretta asked Futelli, "They are both foolth, you thay?"

Futelli replied, "But listen to what they say. It will entertain you."

Piero said to her, "Don shall begin."

He then said to Guzman, "Begin, Don. She has surveyed your outwards and your inwards, through the tears and wounds of your apparel."

"She is politic," Guzman the Spaniard said. "My outside, lady, shrouds an obscured prince."

Amoretta said, "I thank ye for your muthic, pwinth."

Guzman the Spaniard thought, *My words are music to her.*

Amoretta continued, "The muthic and the thong you thent me by thith whithling thing, your man."

Guzman the Spaniard thought, *She has mistaken Fulgoso for my serving-man! God of Love, thou have been just.*

Fulgoso the Parvenu thought, *I will not stay quiet! To be mistaken for his serving-man! It is time to speak before my time.*

He said out loud, "Oh, scurvy! I the serving-man of this man, who has no means for food or even ragged clothing, and who has tears in his clothing seams!"

Guzman said, "I have with this one rapier —"

Piero interrupted, "He has no other."

Guzman the Spaniard continued, "— passed through a field of pikes, whose heads I lopped as easily as the bloody-minded youth lopped off the poppy heads —"

Sextus Tarquinius sent a messenger to ask his father, Tarquinius Superbus (the last king of Rome) how he could conquer the city of Gabii. His father, who was in his garden, took out his sword and decapitated the tallest flowers. Sextus Tarquinius understood that to mean that he should kill the most important men in the city.

Fulgoso the Parvenu said, "The puppet-heads."

Don Quixote attacked some puppets in the belief that they were Moors.

Guzman the Spaniard sputtered, "Have I ... have I ... have I —"

He meant: Have I attacked puppets?

Fulgoso the Parvenu said, "Thou lie, thou have not, and I'll maintain it."

Fulgoso meant that Guzman had not passed through a field of pikes, whose heads he had lopped.

Guzman the Spaniard said, "Have I — but let that pass, for even if my famous acts were damned to silence, yet my descent shall crown me thy superior."

Amoretta, who was interested in high birth, said, "That I would lithen to."

Guzman the Spaniard said, "Listen and wonder. My great-great-grandsire was an ancient duke. He was given the name Desver di Gonzado."

The Spanish word "*desvergonzado*" means "shameless."

Futelli said to Amoretta, "That's, in Spanish, an incorrigible rogue without a fellow — an unmatched rogue. Guzman thinks we don't understand that."

Guzman the Spaniard said, "My grandfather was hight [was called] Argozile."

Futelli said to Amoretta, "He was an arrant, arrant thief-leader. Please note — and mock — it."

Guzman the Spaniard said, "My grandsire by the mother's side was a *conde*: Conde Scrivano."

A *conde* is a Spanish count.

Futelli said to Amoretta, "He was a crop-eared scrivener."

A punishment of the time was to crop — cut off the top of — an offender's ears.

A scrivener was a scribe: someone who copied or wrote documents for pay.

Guzman the Spaniard continued, "Whose son, my mother's father, was a marquis: Hijo di puto."

Hijo di puto is Spanish for "son of a bitch."

Piero said to Amoretta, "That's the son of a whore."

Guzman the Spaniard said, "And my renowned sire, Don Picaro —"

The Spanish *picaro* means "rogue."

Futelli said to Amoretta, "In the proper sense, that means a rascal."

He then said, louder, "Oh, brave Don!"

Guzman the Spaniard said, "Hijo di una pravada —"

Piero said, "He goes on. The name means 'Son of a branded bitch.'"

Criminals could be branded.

Piero then said, louder, "High-spirited Don!"

Guzman the Spaniard said, "He had honors both by sea and land, to wit —"

Futelli said to Amoretta, "The galleys and Bridewell."

The honors by sea were being forced to row a galley-ship. The honors by land were being sentenced to serve a prison term in Bridewell Prison in London.

Fulgoso the Parvenu said, "I'll not endure it. To hear a canting mongrel — "Hear me, lady!"

Guzman the Spaniard objected, "It is no fair play."

Fulgoso the Parvenu said, "I don't care whether it's fair or foul."

He wanted his turn to describe his heritage.

He continued, "I from a king derive my pedigree. King Oberon was his name, from whom my father, the mighty and courageous Mountibanco, was lineally descended; and my mother — in right of whose blood I must always honor the lower Germany — was a Harlequin."

Oberon is King of the Fairies in Shakespeare's *A Midsummer Night's Dream.*

A mountebank is a wandering showman who sells quack medicine.

A harlequin is a buffoon or a Fool (jester) in traditional pantomime.

Futelli said, "He'll blow up Guzman the Spaniard presently by his mother's side."

His mother's side came from "Lower Germany," which is sometimes used to refer to the Low Countries or Netherlands.

Fulgoso the Parvenu continued, "Her father was Grave Hans Van Heme, the son of Hogen Mogen, dat de droates did sneighen of veirteen hundred Spaniards in one neict."

"*Hogen mogen*" are Dutch words meaning, roughly, "high mightinesses."

Out of patriotism, Fulgoso had used a heavy Dutch accent for part of the sentence. He meant: "... that the throats did cut of fourteen hundred Spaniards in one night."

Or, possibly, he had used a heavy Dutch accent in an attempt to keep Guzman the Spaniard from understanding what he was saying.

Guzman the Spaniard said, "Oh, *diabolo*!"

Diablo is Spanish for "devil."

Fulgoso the Parvenu said, "Neither ten thousand devils nor ten thousand *diabolos* shall frighten me from reciting my pedigree.

"My uncle, Yacob Van Flagon-drought [drink from a flagon], with Abraham Snortenfert [snort and fart], and youngster Brogen-foh [brag and fight], with fourscore hargubush [portable guns], managed by well-lined butter-boxes [butter-loving Dutchmen], took a thousand Spanish jobbernowls [blockheads] by surprise, and beat a sconce about their ears."

A sconce can be 1) a lantern, 2) a candlestick, 3) a head, or 4) a small fort.

Guzman the Spaniard said, "My fury is now but justice on thy forfeit life."

He was so angry because of Fulgoso's words against the Spanish that he felt justified in killing Fulgoso.

He drew his sword.

Amoretta said, "Alath ... they thall not fight."

Her words were ambiguous. She was sorrowful either because they would fight and she did not want them to, or she was sorrowful because she knew that they would not fight.

"Fear not, sweet lady," Futelli said.

Piero said to Fulgoso and Guzman, "Be advised, great spirits."

Fulgoso the Parvenu said, "My fortunes bid me to be wise in duels. Or else, hang it, who cares?"

If Fulgoso and Guzman fought a duel and Fulgoso died, he would lose his life and a fortune. But if Guzman died, he would lose only his life. It did not make good economic sense for Fulgoso to fight a duel.

Guzman the Spaniard said, "My honor is my tutor, already tried and known."

"Why, there's the point," Fulgoso the Parvenu said. "My honor is my tutor, too. Noblemen fight in their own persons! I scorn it! It is out of fashion. There's none but harebrained youths of mettle who do it."

The word "mettle" means "character."

Piero said, "Yet don't put up your swords; it is the pleasure of the fair lady that you quit the field with brandished blades in hand."

Futelli said, "And in addition, to show your suffering valor, as her equal favorites, you both should take a competence of kicks. Each of you should get your fair share of kicks."

Guzman the Spaniard and Fulgoso the Parvenu said, "What!"

Futelli and Piero said as they kicked them: "Like this! And this! Go away, you pair of stinkards!"

Fulgoso the Parvenu said, "Phew! As it were."

He whistled.

Guzman the Spaniard said, "Why, since it is her pleasure, I dare and will endure it."

Fulgoso the Parvenu said, "Phew!"

Honor demanded that Fulgoso and Guzman fight Futelli and Piero, but Fulgoso and Guzman were unwilling to do that.

Piero said, "Go away, but stay below."

As a verb, the word "below" can mean "humble yourself and bring yourself low." As an adjective, it can mean "unworthy of."

"Stay below" can mean, of course, stay at a lower level. Currently, they may be in a room on the second floor of Trelcatio's house.

Futelli said, "Budge not, I order you both, until you have further leave."

Guzman the Spaniard said, "My honor claims the last foot in the field."

Fulgoso the Parvenu said, "I'll lead the vanguard — the front part of the army — then."

"Yet more?" Futelli said. "Go away now!"

Fulgoso and Guzman exited.

"Aren't these precious suitors?" Futelli said.

Trelcatio entered the room and asked, "What tumults frighten the house?"

Futelli said, "There was a pair of castrels — hunting hawks — that fluttered, sir, about this lovely game, your daughter, but they dared not give the souse and so they took to hedge."

A "souse" is the swooping of a bird at its prey.

A bird will hide in a hedge in order to be safe.

Piero said, "Mere haggards, buzzards, kites."

These are kinds of birds.

Amoretta said, "I thcorn thuch trumpery; and will thape my luff henthforth ath thall my father betht direct me."

A luff is a front sail. Amoretta was saying that she would from now on take her father's advice.

The practical joke of Futelli and Piero seemed to have worked. Amoretta had said that she was willing to obey her father, who was more sensible than she.

Trelcatio said, "Why now thou sing in tune, my Amoretta —"

He then said to Futelli and Piero, "And, my good friends, you have, like wise physicians, prescribed a healthful diet: I shall think on a bounty for your pains, and will present you to noble Auria, such as your descents — and deserts — commend, but for the present we must leave this room to privacy; they are coming —"

Amoretta said, "Please don't leave me, dentlemen."

Futelli said, "We are your servants."

They exited.

Lord Auria, Lord Adurni, and Aurelio gathered together to talk about what had or had not happened when Lord Adurni was alone with Spinella, Lord Auria's wife.

Each man had an agenda. Lord Auria wanted to clear his wife's name. Lord Adurni wanted to avoid trouble with Lord Auria. Aurelio wanted to justify his actions to Lord Auria, and he wanted to remain friends with Lord Auria.

Of course, Lord Auria wanted to avoid trouble: Trouble would make it difficult to clear his wife's name.

Lord Auria said to Lord Adurni, "You're welcome, be assured you are; for proof, retrieve the boldness — as you please to term it — of visit to commands."

There were two "visits to commands": 1) Lord Auria had become powerful and had requested that Lord Adurni and Aurelio come to visit him. When a powerful man requests something, that request is often treated as a command. Another lord — that is, another powerful man — might object to this kind of request as "bold." 2) Lord Adurni had requested that Spinella come to visit him, and when he was with her alone, he may have made his own "bold" request, whether of social intercourse or of sexual intercourse.

Lord Auria could avoid the charge of boldness by giving power to Lord Adurni — power such as having Aurelio leave the room.

Lord Auria, who wanted to keep the peace between him and Lord Adurni and to clear Spinella's name was inviting Lord Adurni to retrieve — take back in some way — something such as a bad interpretation of what had happened during Spinella's visit to him.

Lord Auria continued, "If this man's presence isn't useful, dismiss him."

"This man" was Aurelio. If Lord Adurni wanted Aurelio to leave, Lord Auria would tell Aurelio to leave. This let Aurelio know that he was the least important man present.

Lord Adurni said, "It is important, if you don't mind, my lord, that your friend witness how far my reputation stands engaged to noble reconcilement."

He wanted to be reconciled to Lord Auria. With good reason, he believed that Lord Auria was angry at him.

Lord Adurni was also willing for Aurelio to be present.

Lord Auria said, "I observe no party here among us who can challenge a motion of such honor. No one here can object to friends being reconciled."

This let Aurelio know that Lord Auria wanted to be reconciled to Lord Adurni.

Lord Adurni said, "Even if your looks could borrow clearer serenity and calmness than can the peace of a composed soul, yet I presume that report of my attempt, trained by a curiosity in youth for scattering clouds before them, has raised tempests that will at last break out."

Lord Auria looked very calm, but even if Lord Auria could look calmer, which would be difficult, Lord Adurni worried that gossip about his attempt to do something not yet specified would have made Lord Auria angry and that his anger would eventually break out.

Some of what Lord Adurni had said was ambiguous.

This is one meaning:

I presume that report of my attempt at the seduction of your wife, which was a result of a trap I set because my youth made me want to acquire knowledge of what it would be like to have sex with her although such a desire for knowledge I ought not to have has had the result of gossip-scattering clouds that obscure clear serenity and calmness and the peace of a composed soul.

This is another meaning

I presume that Aurelio's misleading report of my attempt at providing especially good hospitality, a report that was brought about because Aurelio, who was paying too much attention when keeping an eye on your wife and who was overly curious about what was happening between your wife and me behind closed doors, character traits that he apparently learned in youth, had the result of gossip-spreading clouds that obscure clear serenity and calmness and the peace of a composed soul.

These clouds in turn had formed storm clouds in Lord Auria's mind.

When Lord Auria learned more about the attempt, not yet specified in words, Lord Auria's storm clouds, now hidden, might entirely break out in violence.

Lord Auria said, "Those storm clouds are hidden now, most likely, in the darkness of your speech."

The speech was dark in part because it was not clearly expressed. Also, the speech could very well be about seduction or attempted seduction.

Lord Adurni was feeling his way in the situation, deciding how best to proceed.

Aurelio said, "You may be plainer."

He meant: You may speak more clearly and plainly.

But the word "plain," when applied to non-material things such as power and justice, also means, according to the *Oxford English Dictionary*, "full, complete, entire; perfect, absolute."

Aurelio, therefore, was saying, "You may be more just."

Lord Adurni replied, "I shall."

He then said to Lord Auria, "My lord, that I intended wrong —"

Lord Auria said, "Ha! Wrong! To whom?"

Lord Adurni said, "To Auria, and as far as language could prevail, did —"

This conversation was dangerous. Lord Auria wanted to clear his wife's name, not fight a duel with Lord Adurni. If Lord Adurni admitted to committing a certain type of wrong against Lord Auria, they would fight. Lord Auria wished to avoid a duel, but he was a brave and honorable man. If honor demanded that he fight, he would fight.

Lord Auria interrupted, "Take my advice, young lord, before thy tongue betray a secret concealed yet from the world.

"Hear and consider: In all my flight of vanity and giddiness, when the wings of my excess were scarcely fledged, when a bodily disturbance of youthful heat might have excused disorder and ambition, even then, and so from thence until now the down of softness is exchanged for plumes of confirmed and hardened age, I never dared pitch on any howsoever likely rest, where the presumption might be construed as the doing of wrong."

Lord Auria was now a mature man, while Lord Adurni was a young man. Lord Auria was saying that ever since he was a young man and his youthful heat, or lust, might have excused some not-so-good behavior, even then, and up until now, he had avoided any kind of behavior and rest that could lead people to think that he was committing a sin.

One meaning of "to pitch" is "to thrust in," as in driving a stake or nail into a solid body.

"Pitching behavior" can include sex.

The noun "rest" can mean a resting space for something. A penis can rest in a vagina during a pause between strenuous bouts of activity. Also, the bolt of a gate is slid into what this society called a "rest," aka socket.

Rest can take place in bed after strenuous activity.

The words also continued the bird metaphor. The verb "pitch" can mean to "alight on the ground." Birds can enjoy rest.

Lord Auria continued, "The word 'wrong' is hateful, and the sense wants pardon."

Actions that are morally right do not want pardon: They don't need it.

Lord Auria continued, "For, as I dared not wrong the meanest, so he who but only aimed by any boldness a wrong to me, would find I must not bear it: The one is as unmanly as the other."

In other words: Be careful what you admit. If you admit the wrong thing, I will fight you. The wrong need not actually be accomplished, but only aimed at — intended.

He then said, "Now, continue without interruption."

Lord Adurni said, "Stand, Aurelio, and justify thine accusation boldly. Spare me the needless use of my confession."

This is intelligent. First let it clearly be said what you are accused of, and then respond to it. Otherwise, you may find yourself talking about wrongs you have not been accused of.

Lord Adurni continued, "And, having told no more than what thy jealousy possessed thee with, again before my face urge to thy friend — Auria — the breach of hospitality Lord Adurni trespassed in, and thou conceived, against Spinella."

Here Lord Adurni was referring to two breaches of hospitality: the breach of hospitality that Lord Adurni trespassed in, and the breach of hospitality that Aurelio conceived in his imagination.

Lord Adurni could be thinking that his breach of hospitality was what Spinella had called it when speaking earlier to Malfato. Spinella had said about Lord Adurni: "He was in excess of entertainment; otherwise, he was not importunately wanton."

The breach of hospitality that Aurelio had conceived in his imagination was actual or attempted seduction. Aurelio's suspicion had led to his breaking into the room in which were Lord Adurni and Spinella, and this had in turn caused gossip and loss of reputation.

Lord Adurni then said, "Why, evidence grows faint if barely not supposed I'll answer guilty."

In other words, the only way that Aurelio can succeed in proving his accusation is if Lord Adurni were to plead guilty to it. If there is even a small chance that Lord Adurni will not plead guilty, then all the evidence that Aurelio has will grow faint. No confession, no conviction.

Aurelio asked, "Haven't you come here to defy and threaten us?"

"No, Aurelio," Lord Adurni said. "I have come here only to reply upon that brittle evidence to which thy cunning never shall rejoin — despite your cunning, you shall never make a satisfactory reply to my charge that your evidence is weak.

"I make my judge my jury."

Aurelio had already judged Lord Adurni guilty of one thing, but Lord Adurni wanted him to be the jury and decide the answer to something else.

Lord Adurni identified that task for the jury: "Decide whether, with all the eagerness of spleen or a suspicious rage can plead, thou have driven the likelihood of scandal."

Certainly, Aurelio's breaking into the private chamber in which Lord Adurni and Spinella were alone had resulted in much scandal concerning Spinella.

Aurelio said, "Don't doubt that I have delivered the honest truth, as much as I believe and justly witness."

People can believe something that is false.

Lord Adurni said, "Those are weak foundations on which to raise a bulwark of reproach! And thus for that!

"My errand in coming here is not, in whining, truant-like submission, to cry, 'I have offended; please, forgive me. I won't do it any more.'

"Instead, my purpose is only to proclaim the power of virtue, whose commanding rule and power set bounds and checks on rebel bloods.

"The power of virtue restrains the habits of folly.

"By the use of example, the power of virtue teaches a rule to reformation.

"By the use of rewards, the power of virtue crowns worthy actions and gives invitations to honor."

Aurelio said, "Honor and worthy actions best become their lips who practice both, and don't lecture about them."

Lord Auria said, "Peace! Peace, man!"

He wanted the two men to talk, not fight.

He then said, "I am silent."

Lord Adurni said, "Some there are, and they are not few in number, who resolve no beauty can be chaste unless unattempted."

This is a cynical view. It means that any beautiful woman will be unchaste when someone tries to commit adultery with her.

But Lord Adurni might have meant that some people believe that no beauty can be chaste unless attempted.

In this case, acquiring the virtue of chastity involves resisting one or more attempts at convincing the beauty to commit adultery and be unchaste.

Lord Adurni continued, "And, because the liberty of courtship flies from the wanton to the her who comes next, meeting oftentimes too many soon seduced, conclude all may be won by gifts, by service, or compliments of vows."

A seducer will seduce a wanton woman and then move on to the next woman. The seducer will find many women who are easily seduced, and because he finds many women who are seduced with gifts, deeds, and words, he concludes that all women can be seduced with gifts, deeds, and words.

But does the seduction necessarily have to be immortal? The deeds could include courtship. In that case, the seduction would be to persuade the woman to marry the man and have chaste — moral — sex.

Lord Adurni continued, "And with this file I stood in rank; conquest secured my confidence."

He was perhaps admitting openly to being a seducer and to having seduced many women. In that case, the conquest referred to was his conquest.

Or he was admitting openly to his belief that all women could be seduced — to either a moral seduction or an immoral seduction. In that case, the conquest referred to was not his conquest, but that of another man or men.

He continued, "Spinella — don't be angry, Auria — was an object of study for fruition."

"Fruition" means enjoyment. It could refer to 1) the enjoyment of having sex with Spinella, or 2) the enjoyment of finding out that at least one woman is chaste.

Lord Adurni had said only that Spinella was "an object of study," not that he had actually attempted to seduce her.

He continued, "Here I angled, not doubting the deceit could find resistance."

The word "deceit" can mean 1) lie, or 2) trick.

The word "doubting" can mean "fearing" in this society, or it can have its usual meaning.

If he did not doubt that the deceit could find resistance, he knew that the deceit could find resistance.

If he did not fear that the deceit could find resistance, he knew that the deceit could not find resistance.

Lord Adurni had either attempted to seduce Spinella, or he had set up a trick in order to prove that she was chaste.

Aurelio said, "After confession follows —"

Aurelio believed that Lord Adurni had just confessed to attempted seduction.

Lord Auria said, "Noise! Observe him."

This meant: Don't interrupt. Pay attention to Lord Adurni.

Lord Adurni had not actually confessed to seduction or attempted seduction.

Lord Adurni said, "Oh, strange! By all the comforts of my hopes, I found a woman good — a woman good!"

He did not say how he had found her good. Was it through her rejection of an attempted seduction, or was what might appear to be an attempted seduction only a trick to test her?

He continued, "Yet, as I wish belief, or desire an honorable reputation, so much majesty of humbleness and scorn appeared at once in fair, in chaste, in wise Spinella's eyes that I grew dull in utterance, and one frown from her cooled every flame of sensual appetite—"

Lord Adurni paused, wondering whether he had said too much, but even when a man intends only to test a woman's chastity, the man's sensual appetite can be aroused.

Lord Auria said, "Go on, sir, and do not stop."

Lord Adurni said, "Without protests, I pleaded merely love."

"Love" can mean 1) fondness and affection, or 2) sexual desire.

He continued, "I used no syllables except those a virgin might without a blush have listened to, and, not well equipped to resist, have pitied."

Such syllables and such pity could be entirely innocent or could lead a virgin to bed.

Lord Adurni continued, "But she, ignoring my words, cried, 'Come, Auria, come. Fight for thy wife at home!'"

He said to Aurelio, "Then in rushed you, sir. You talked in much fury, and then departed. As soon as you left, the lady vanished, and the rest left after her."

Lord Auria said, "What happened next?"

Lord Adurni's commission here had been to examine his fault and to make a judgment about it. His fault had been his behavior regarding Spinella.

Lord Adurni said, "My commission on my error, in execution whereof I have proved myself to be so exact in every point, that I renounce all memory, not to this one fault alone, but to my other greater and more irksome fault."

He was saying that his fault was minor and not worth remembering.

The same applied to his "other greater and more irksome fault," which was probably his affair with Levidolce, and other affairs. Indeed, having that fault known and remembered would hurt Levidolce. People would regard her as a wanton woman.

Of course, Spinella and Lord Auria wanted to restore Spinella's reputation lest she be labeled a wanton woman.

Lord Adurni continued, "Now let any man who owns a name and is of good birth and who construes this testimony of mine the report of fear, of falsehood or imposture, tell me that I give myself the lie."

He was giving Lord Auria and Aurelio the chance to object to what he had said. They did not have to object, but now was their opportunity to do so.

Lord Adurni believed what he had said: His faults were minor and ought not to be remembered.

If Lord Adurni were told that he gives himself the lie, he would be told that he was lying to himself. Being told that one was a liar was a serious offense and required the fighting of a duel.

Lord Adurni continued, "If he tells me that, I will clear the injury."

He could do that by fighting and winning the duel.

He continued, "And man to man, or if such justice may prove doubtful, two to two, or three to three, or any way needed I will reprieve the opinion of my forfeit without blemish."

"To reprieve" means "to redeem" or "to bring back."

A "forfeit" is a misdeed.

Lord Adurni had talked about his misdeeds and had said that they were not serious enough to be remembered, and if anyone thought he had lied, he would get back the opinion that his misdeeds were not serious enough to be remembered.

He would win the duel, whether it was one against one, or two against two, or three against three, and by doing so, he would show himself innocent of lying.

Angry at the mention of dueling, Lord Auria said, "Who can you think I am? Did you expect so great a tameness and meekness that you find, Lord Adurni, that you can cast loud defiance? Say —"

His anger sprang from knowing that there was no need to talk about dueling. Talking about it made it more likely to happen.

Lord Auria had spoken up quickly, before Aurelio could speak up. Lord Auria did not want Lord Adurni and Aurelio to fight a duel.

Lord Adurni said, "I have robbed you of severity, Lord Auria, by my strict self-penance for the presumption."

He believed that Lord Auria could wish, or could have wished, to fight a duel with him, but that his testimony had robbed him of that. Any duel would be fought between Lord Adurni and someone else.

Lord Adurni had mentioned a duel of two against two, or three against three. He had offered that in case people believed that a duel of one against one would make justice doubtful, as when one man was clearly superior to the other in dueling.

Lord Auria had recently distinguished himself in military matters.

Lord Auria said, "Surely, Italians hardly admit dispute in questions of this nature. The trick is new."

In other words, no duel was needed here.

Lord Adurni said, "I find my absolution by vows of change from all ignoble practice."

He was vowing to refrain from all ignoble practice. He would avoid doing evil. He was vowing to reform. This is something that both Lord Auria and Aurelio would approve of.

Lord Auria said, "Why, look, friend, I told you this before, but you would not be persuaded."

Lord Auria had previously advised Lord Adurni to reform, but he had not reformed.

Walking apart from the others, Lord Auria said, "Let me think —"

He still wanted to achieve his objective: He wanted to clear Spinella's name and reputation.

Aurelio said to Lord Adurni, "You do not yet deny that you solicited the lady to ill purpose. You haven't denied that you attempted to seduce her."

Lord Adurni avoided the question by saying, "I have already answered that. But it returned much quiet to my mind, perplexed with rare commotions."

Lord Auria said to himself, "That's the way. It overcomes all obstacles."

He had decided on a course of action.

Overhearing, Aurelio said, "My lord?"

Lord Auria said, "Bah! I am thinking —

"You may continue to talk."

He then continued to talk to himself, "If it takes, it is clear. And then — and then — and so — and so —"

Lord Adurni said, "You labor with curious engines — ingenious devices — surely."

"Fine ones!" Lord Auria said, "I take you to be a man of credit; else —"

"Suspicion is needless," Lord Adurni said. "You should know me better than that."

"Yet you must not part from me, sir," Lord Auria said.

"As for that, I am at your pleasure," Lord Adurni said.

Lord Auria quoted what he had been told his wife had said: "'Come, fight for thy wife at home, my Auria!'"

He then said, "Yes, we can fight, my Spinella, when thine honor relies upon a champion."

He would be that champion.

Trelcatio entered the room.

Lord Auria asked, "What is it now?"

Trelcatio replied, "My lord, Castanna, along with her sister and Malfato, have just arrived."

Lord Auria said to Trelcatio, "Don't be loud. Escort them into the gallery."

He then said, "Aurelio, friend, and Lord Adurni, lord, we three will sit in council, and piece together a heartfelt league of friendship among us, or scuffle harshly."

CHAPTER 5

— 5.1 —

Martino, Benazzi, and Levidolce talked together in a room in Martino's house. Benazzi and Levidolce had entered Martino's house, and Martino had no idea who Benazzi was: He thought that Benazzi was a bandit and that he and Levidolce had come to rob and murder him. Benazzi still dressed like and looked like a bandit, and so Martino did not recognize him.

Martino said, "Ruffian, get out of my house! Thou have come to rob me.

"Police! Help!

"My house is haunted by a vulgar pack of thieves, harlots, murderers, rogues, and vagabonds!

"I foster and care for a decoy here, and she trolls on her ragged customer to cut my throat for pillage."

The decoy was Levidolce, whom he had reared and whom he thought had lured him into a trap in which he would be murdered and robbed.

"To troll" can mean 1) "to move the tongue nimbly," or 2) "to move with a rolling action."

Martino was saying that Levidolce had urged the bandit to rob him, and he was implying that she had moved sexually in bed with the bandit.

The ragged customer was Benazzi.

In this society, "customer" could mean companion, but Martino was now and would continue to insult Levidolce by both implying and openly stating that she was a whore.

"Good sir, hear me," Levidolce said.

Benazzi said, "Hear or not hear — let him rave his lungs out!

"While this woman has abode under this roof, I will justify myself as her bedfellow in despite of denial — in despite: Those are my words."

"Monstrous!" Martino said to Benazzi. "What, sirrah, do I keep a bawdy-house? Do I keep a hospital for panders?"

He then said to Levidolce, "Oh, thou monster! Thou she-confusion! Thou female bringer of ruin and destruction! Have you grown so unrestrained that, from a private wanton, thou proclaim thyself a baggage for all gamesters, lords or gentlemen, strangers or home-spun yeomen, footposts, pages, roarers, or hangmen?"

"Roarers" were roaring boys who drank and fought.

She had had an affair with Lord Adurni; now Martino was accusing her of being a prostitute who would sleep with anyone.

Martino then said, "Hey! Set up shop, and then cry, 'This market is open, go to it, and welcome!'"

"This is my husband," Levidolce said.

"Husband!" Martino said.

Benazzi said, "I am her natural husband. I have married her, and what's your verdict on the match, signor?"

"Husband, and married her!" Martino said.

"Indeed, it is the truth," Levidolce said.

To Martino, it seemed as if his great-niece had married a bandit.

Martino said sarcastically, "A proper joining! A fine marriage! May God give you joy, great mistress. Your fortunes are advanced, indeed, are they? What jointure is assured, please tell me? Some three thousand each year in oaths and vermin? A fair advancement!"

A jointure is an estate for a wife to live on if her husband dies.

Martino continued, "Was there ever such a tattered rag of man's flesh patched up for copesmate to my great-niece's daughter!"

A copesmate is 1) a marriage partner, 2) a partner in cheating and swindling, 3) a paramour, and/or 4) an enemy.

Levidolce said, "Sir, for my mother's name forbear this anger: Even if I have yoked myself beneath your wishes, my choice is still a lawful one, and I will live as truly chaste to his bosom as ever my faith has bound me."

Not convinced, Martino said, "A sweet couple!"

"We are a sweet couple," Benazzi said.

He had been a soldier, and as such, he had protected people such as Martino; he regarded himself as a worthy husband for Levidolce.

Benazzi said, "As for my own part, although my outside appears shabby, I have wrestled with death, Signor Martino, in order to preserve your sleeps, and such as you are, untroubled.

"A soldier is a mockery in peacetime, a very town bull for laughter."

The unemployed soldiers are treated like town fools and are laughed at. A "bull" is a ludicrous jest.

Benazzi continued, "Curmudgeons lay their baits for traps to prey on unthrifts and landed babies."

"Unthrifts" are people who do not thrive, and "landed babies" are needy soldiers who have landed on the shores of Britain after fighting overseas. Many returned soldiers are vulnerable and dependent and so they are metaphorical babies.

Benazzi continued, "Let the wars rattle about your ears once, and the security of a soldier is very honorable among you then! That day may shine again. So let's get on to my business."

Martino said, "A soldier! Thou a soldier! I do believe thou are lousy; that's a pretty sign, I grant."

"Lousy" means "lice-ridden." Staying lice-free is difficult for soldiers fighting during wars, as it is for bandits living rough in wooded areas.

Martino continued, "You are a villainous, poor *bandito* rather, one who can man a whore, and speak the cant of thieves and beggars, and pick a pocket, walk softly after a man wearing a cloak or hat so you can steal it, and in the dark use a pistol to shoot a straggler for a quarter-ducat."

A quarter-ducat is a very small amount of money.

Martino continued, "A soldier! Yes — he looks as if he lacks the spirit of a herring or a tumbler."

Herrings are smoked, and one meaning of the verb "smoke" is to be angry or to fume.

A tumbler is 1) a species of hound that was used to catch rabbits, or 2) a person who lures someone into the hands of swindlers.

Benazzi said, "Let age and dotage rage together!

"Levidolce, thou are mine. On what conditions thou are mine, the world shall soon witness. Since our hands joined in betrothal, I have not yet exercised my right to the possession of thy bed; nor until I have carried out thy injunction to me do I intend to exercise my right."

Levidolce had asked him to do something for her, and he had agreed. After he had done it, he would consummate their new marriage.

Benazzi said to her, "Kiss me quickly and resolutely!"

She kissed him, and he said, "Good!"

He then said to Martino, "Adieu, signor!"

Levidolce said, "Dear, for love's sake, stay."

Benazzi replied, "Don't ask me to stay."

He exited, leaving Martino and Levidolce alone together.

Martino said, "Ah, thou — but what? I don't know what to call thee. I would eagerly smother grief, but it must come out. My heart is broken. Thou have for many a day been at a loss, and now thou are lost forever — lost, lost, without recovery."

Levidolce said, "With your pardon, let me restrain and hold back your sorrows."

Martino replied, "It is impossible. Despair of rising up to honest reputation turns all the courses wild, and this last action will roar thy infamy and bad reputation."

"This last action" was a bad marriage — a marriage to a bandit. He believed that she had married the bandit because she believed that she had lost her good reputation and could marry no one better.

He hesitated and then asked, "Then you are certainly married, indeed, to this newcomer?"

"Yes," Levidolce said, "and herein every hope is brought to life that long has lain in deadness; I have once more wedded Benazzi, my divorced husband."

"Benazzi!" Martino said. "This man is Benazzi?"

Levidolce said, "No odd disguise could guard him from discovery: I recognized him. This man is he, the choice of my ambition; may heaven keep me always thankful for such a bounty!

"So far he dreams not of this deceit — I have kept secret my recognition of him.

"But let me die in speaking, if I don't believe that my success is happier than any earthly blessing.

"Oh, sweet great-uncle, rejoice with me! I am a faithful convert, and I will use love and true obedience to redeem the stains of a foul name. "

Martino said, "The force of passion shows me to be a child again."

He was crying from happiness. Levidolce had remarried her former husband whom she had divorced, and she had vowed to reform.

He continued, "Do, Levidolce, perform thy resolutions; once those are performed, I have been only steward for your welfare. You shall have all between you."

Levidolce and Benazzi would get all of his wealth.

Levidolce said, "Join with me, sir. Our plot requires much speed; we must be earnest. I'll tell you what conditions threaten danger unless you intervene. Let us hasten, for fear we come too late."

Levidolce had something big planned.

Martino said, "Since thou intend to reform and acquire a virtuous honesty, I am thy supporter in anything you want me to do, witty Levidolce, my great-niece, my witty great-niece."

"Witty" means "intelligent."

Levidolce said, "Let's waste no time, sir."

— 5.2 —

Trelcatio, Malfato, Spinella, and Castanna met together in an apartment in Trelcatio's house.

Trelcatio said, "Kinsman and ladies, have a little patience. All will be as you wish; I guarantee it. Fear nothing; Auria is a noble fellow. I leave you, but know that I will be within hearing distance. Take courage."

He exited.

"Courage!" an unhappy Malfato said. "They who have no hearts find no hearts and courage to lose; ours is as great as that of the man who defies danger most.

"Surely, state and ceremony inhabit here. Like strangers, we shall await a formal reception."

They were close friends and relatives to Lord Auria and ought to be given a friendly, not a formal, reception.

Malfato said to Spinella, "Cousin, let us return to my house; this treatment of us is paltry."

Spinella said, "Gentle sir, restrain your passion; only I have the duty to be here."

Castanna said, "Now, for heaven's sake, sister!"

Lord Auria and Aurelio entered the room.

Castanna said, "He comes — your husband comes. Take comfort, sister."

"Malfato!" Lord Auria said.

"Auria!" Malfato said.

Lord Auria embraced Malfato and then replied, "Cousin, I wish that my arms in their embraces might at once deliver affectionately what interest your merit holds in my estimation!"

In other words, Lord Auria was telling Malfato that he regarded him highly.

"I may chide the shyness of this intercourse between us that a retired privacy on your part has pleased to show."

In other words, Lord Auria was telling Malfato that he regretted that the two were not closer. Malfato had been keeping to himself rather than sometimes meeting with Lord Auria.

103

Most likely, the reason was that Lord Auria had married the woman Malfato loved.

Lord Auria added, "If I can do anything that would cause you to have a kind opinion of me, I shall honor the means and practice — I will do it."

"That 'anything' is your charity and love," Malfato said.

"Worthy Malfato!" Aurelio said.

"Provident Aurelio!" Malfato said.

"Castanna, virtuous maiden!" Lord Auria said.

"I am your servant, brother-in-law," Castanna said.

Spinella knelt before Lord Auria.

Lord Auria asked, "But who's that other?"

"That other" was his wife: Spinella. Lord Auria was asking this question because his wife was kneeling before him. He preferred a more equal relationship.

Lord Auria said, "Such a face my eyes have been acquainted with; the sight resembles something that is not quite lost to remembrance.

"Why does the lady kneel? To whom does she kneel?

"Please rise. I shall forget my civil manners because of imagining that you tender to me a false tribute, or because of imagining that the man to whom you tender it is a counterfeit — an imposter."

How could Lord Auria be a counterfeit — an imposter? He was a loving husband, but he would not seem sometimes to be a loving husband during this "trial" of his wife. Yet all he was doing was done for the purpose of restoring his wife's reputation.

Spinella's kneeling to him could be a "false tribute" in that he would seem to be persecuting her at times although everything he did was intended to clear her name.

His wife rose.

Malfato objected to Lord Auria's pretending not to know his own wife; of course, Lord Auria knew his own wife! Pretending not to know her seemed to be putting on a show of power over her.

Malfato said, "My lord, you use a borrowed bravery that does not lead to generous interpretations. May your fortunes mount higher than apprehension can reach them!"

Lord Auria did not seem to be acting intelligently, and so Malfato wished that his fortunes in life would prove to be better than his intelligence.

Malfato continued, "Yet this waste kind of antic sovereignty over a wife who equals the best of your deserts, achievements, or prosperity, reveals a barrenness of noble nature. Let upstarts exercise uncomely roughness and rudeness; clear spirits to the humble will be humble. You know your wife, no doubt."

Of course, Malfato meant "know" in the sense of "recognize," but the Biblical "know" means to "know sexually."

Lord Auria used sexual puns in his answer to Malfato:

"I cry for your mercy, gentleman!

"Probably, you have come to tutor a good carriage, and are expert in the nick of it. We shall study your instructions quaintly."

To "tutor a good carriage" means to "teach good manners"; "carriage" can also refer to carrying a man's weight in bed while in the missionary position, and "carriage" can refer to carrying a baby.

The work "nick" means "essential part," and the word "quaintly" means "assiduously."

The word "nick" can refer to the vulva, and the word "quaint" can also refer to the vulva.

Lord Auria continued, "You said, 'Wife'? I agree to that. Continue to be fair, and attend the trial."

This was the first time Spinella had heard the word "trial." She could guess that it was she who was on trial, and this made her angry. What would be a good reason for a husband to put his wife on trial?

Spinella said, "Those words raise a lively soul in her who almost yielded to faintness and numbness. I thank you for that.

"Prove, though, what you will judge; until I can purge objections that require belief and conscience, I have no kindred, sister, husband, friend, or pity for my plea."

Spinella wanted her husband to be a fair judge: one who looked at real evidence. She also knew that she needed to get rid of objections against her — serious objections that were held with belief and conscience. By doing so, she could make herself clean again.

To make clear that she wanted no special considerations during the trial, she said that she would have "no kindred, sister, husband, friend, or pity for my plea."

Malfato said, not to Spinella, "Do you call this a welcome?"

He then said, "We have been mistaken in what we thought would happen here, Castanna."

Castanna said, "Oh, my lord, other things were promised!"

Lord Auria said to his wife, "Lady, did you say, 'No kindred, sister, husband, friend'?"

Spinella said, "Nor name."

She would not have the name of "wife." She would have no title that would come from being the wife of Lord Auria, who was now a lord.

The word "name" also meant "reputation." She did not want her reputation, good or bad, to be used for or against her.

She continued, "With this addition — I disclaim all benefit of mercy from a charitable thought if one or all of the subtleties of malice, if any engineer of faithless discord, if supposition for pretense in folly can point out, without injury to goodness, a likelihood of guilt in my behavior that may declare neglect in every duty required, fit, or exacted."

"The subtleties of malice" are "the tricks and schemes that come from the intention to do evil."

"Any engineer of faithless discord" means "anyone who creates perfidious and disloyal disharmony between people" — in this case, between a husband and wife.

"Supposition for pretense in folly" means "assumption of a claim in foolishness" — that is, foolishly assuming something.

In other words, if she were found guilty for whatever reason — and those reasons would be unfair — then let no mercy be shown to her.

Lord Auria said about Spinella and her words, "High and peremptory! The confidence is masculine."

"And why not?" Malfato said. "An honorable cause gives life to truth without control."

"I can proceed," Spinella said.

She had more to say.

She continued, "That tongue whose venom has spread the infection by traducing spotless honor, is not more my enemy than their, or his, weak and besotted brains are on whom the poison of its cankered falsehood has wrought to procure belief in so foul a mischief."

Who were her enemies? One was Aurelio, whose tongue gave voice to words when he broke into the chamber in which Spinella and Lord Adurni were alone. Other enemies were the brains of those on whom Aurelio's poison had worked to produce belief that she was unchaste. As far as she knew, those brains possibly included the brains of her husband, Lord Auria.

Spinella continued, "Speak, sir, you who are the churlish voice of this combustion, Aurelio, speak. And, gentle sir, don't keep back anything that you know, but roundly use your eloquence against a mean defendant."

The word "mean" can mean 1) abject, 2) inferior in rank, 3) inferior in quality, 4) inferior in ability, 5) poor, 6) badly off, and/or 7) debased.

Observing Aurelio, Malfato said, "He's put to it. It seems the challenge gravels him."

Aurelio was under strain and perplexed.

Aurelio said, "The information I gave came from my doubts and fears, not from any actual knowledge I had."

This was an important admission: He had no actual knowledge that seduction or attempted seduction had occurred. He had given information based on surmise.

He continued, "A self-confession of one's faults may ask for assistance."

A person who confesses sins to a priest can ask for absolution. A person can ask another person for forgiveness.

He continued, "Let the lady's justice impose the penance."

A priest can impose penance in the form of such things as saying the Hail Mary prayer. A non-Catholic can impose a different kind of penance.

Aurelio continued, "So, in the rules of friendship as of love, suspicion is not seldom an improper advantage for knitting more firmly fixed joints of the most faithful affection, by the fevers of casualty unloosed, where lastly error has run into the toil."

Suspicion can make relationships, whether of friendship or of love, stronger.

A casualty is an unfortunate occurrence.

Aurelio was saying that once the unfortunate occurrence of suspicion had caused trouble but had then run its course, with the error of unfounded suspicion being combatted and defeated, then relationships could become stronger.

Spinella said, "That is woeful satisfaction for a divorce of hearts!"

A future better relationship was small compensation for what she was going through now: a divorce between her heart and Lord Auria's heart.

Lord Auria said, "Are you so resolute? I shall touch nearer home: Behold these hairs."

His hair was beginning to grow white.

He continued, "They are great masters of a spirit."

John Conington translated Horace's *Carmina*, Book 3, Poem 14, lines 25-26 in this way:

"*Soon palls the taste for noise and fray,*

"*When hair is white and leaves are sere:*"

In other words, white hair has a calming effect on a man: The man no longer wishes for noise and fights.

To some extent, this was true of Lord Auria. He was willing to leave home and fight Turkish pirates, but he wanted quiet and peace at home.

Lord Auria continued speaking to Spinella, with the others listening, "Yet my few white hairs are not by the winter of old age quite hidden in snow, although I must acknowledge that some messengers of time took up lodging among black hairs.

"When we first exchanged our faiths in wedlock, I was proud I had prevailed with one whose youth and beauty deserved a choice more suitable in both."

He was saying that Spinella deserved a husband who was both younger and better looking than he was.

Lord Auria continued, "Advancement to a fortune could not court ambition either on my side or hers."

According to Lord Auria's words, neither he nor his wife had married for money.

Lord Auria continued, "Love drove the bargain, and the truth of love confirmed it, I conceived.

"But disproportion in years among the married is a reason for change of pleasures. To this I reply that our union was not forced, it was by consent, and so then the breach in such a case appears unpardonable."

If Spinella had sought a younger lover because of Lord Auria's age, that would be unpardonable because their match had been a love match. Adultery would be more understandable if she had married him for his money — both knew that she had not done this because he had not been wealthy.

Lord Auria said to Spinella, "Say your thoughts."

Spinella said, "My thoughts in that respect are as resolute as yours; they are the same.

"Yet herein evidence of frailty did not more greatly deserve a separation than does charge of disloyalty objected without either any ground or witness."

The phrase "evidence of frailty" was ambiguous. It could mean 1) evidence that someone had been frail and weak — for example, in resisting the temptation to commit adultery, or 2) the evidence itself is frail and weak.

The "charge of disloyalty objected" was ambiguous. It could mean 1) the charge of objected — hated — disloyalty, 2) the charge of disloyalty objected to — rebuffed. In either case, the phrase "without either any ground or witness" applied.

Spinella's next words referred to two possible faults: one concerning a woman, and one concerning a man. In this context, we can guess that she is referring to these specific faults: 1) a woman who has been accused of infidelity, and 2) a man who believes the accusation without any evidence.

Spinella said, "Women's faults subject to punishments and men's faults applauded prescribe no laws in force."

In other words: No enacted laws prescribe that women's faults be subject to punishments and that men's faults be applauded.

Or: Women's faults subject to punishments and men's faults applauded decree no laws in force.

Any law that subjects women's faults to punishment and men's faults to applause is unfair.

Aurelio asked, "Are you so nimble?"

The word "nimble" can be positive or negative.

A person can defend him- or herself fairly and rationally — or through seeking a loophole.

Malfato said, "A soul purged of dross by competition, such as mighty Auria's soul is famed, descends from its own sphere, when injuries, profound ones, yield to the combat of a scolding mastery: a skirmish of words.

"Has your wife lewdly ranged, adulterating the honor of your bed? If so, then withhold dispute, but execute your vengeance with unresisted rage. We shall look on. Allow that the fact is true, and spurn her from our bloods.

"Otherwise, if proof of infidelity is not detected, you have wronged her innocence unworthily and childishly, for which I challenge satisfaction."

Malfato was willing to fight a duel with Lord Auria on account of Spinella.

Castanna said about Lord Auria, "It is a tyranny to ungently insult a humble and obedient sweetness."

As she talked, Lord Adurni entered the room. He could guess who was being insulted: Spinella.

Lord Adurni said, "That I will make good, and I must without exception find admittance fitting the party who has herein interest."

He meant that he would turn aside that insult and replace it with good. In addition, he would fix things so that the party being insulted would find admittance into the hearts of everyone present.

Lord Adurni said, "Let's assume I was in fault. If I were at fault, then that fault stretched merely to a misguided thought."

If he were at fault, he had committed no faulty action; he had merely thought of actions that were faulty.

He continued, "And who in this room, except the pair of fair and matchless sisters, Spinella and Castanna, can clear themselves of an imputation of similar folly and foolishness?"

He had done nothing that no man present had not also done: He had sinned in his mind.

Lord Adurni continued, "Here I ask your pardon, excellent Spinella. I ask pardon of only you.

"Your pardon being granted to me, then any man among you who calls for an even reckoning shall meet an even accountant."

He was asking for the pardon of Spinella only; once that pardon was granted, if any man still held anything against him, he would fight that man.

Lord Auria said, "Am I being tormented by a conspiracy of people? I must have my right."

Spinella said to Lord Auria, "And I must have my right, my lord. My lord, what trouble and disturbance is here! You can suspect —"

Suspect whom? Spinella.

She continued speaking to her husband, "— and so reconciliation between us, then, is unwanted. Conclude the difference by taking revenge, or by parting, and we shall never more see one another."

She then said, "Sister, lend me thine arm. I have assumed a courage above my power and ability, and I can hold out no longer."

She had pretended to have a strength she did not possess.

She then said, "Auria, unkind! Unkind!"

Spinella collapsed.

"She faints," Castanna said.

Lord Auria picked her up and put her on a couch.

She regained consciousness.

"Spinella!" he said. "Regent of my affections, thou have conquered in this trial. I find thy virtues as I left them, perfect, pure, and unflawed; for instance, let me claim Castanna's promise."

He would show how highly he regarded his wife, Spinella, by doing something good for her sister, Castanna.

"My promise?" Castanna asked.

Lord Auria replied, "Yours, to whose faith I am a guardian, but not by imposition. Instead, you chose me to be your guardian. Look, I have fitted a husband for you, noble and deserving."

The word "fitted" could mean 1) made suitable and fitting, or 2) forced by fits. The word "fits" could mean "the process of fitting."

Lord Auria had made Lord Adurni a suitable husband for Castanna, perhaps through force, or the force of persuasion.

Lord Auria said, "No shrinking back."

Was he speaking to Lord Adurni or to Castanna or to both?

Lord Auria then said, "Lord Adurni, I present Castanna; she will be a wife of worth."

"What's that?" Malfato said.

Lord Adurni said to Lord Auria, "So great a blessing crowns all desires of life."

He then said to Castanna, "This offer of marriage, lady, I can assure you, is not sudden to me; instead, it is welcomed and forethought. I wish that you could please to say the same!"

Lord Auria said, "Castanna, do. Speak, dearest. It rectifies all crooked vain surmises."

Lord Auria was overstating this. True, marriage to Castanna could help rectify things. If Lord Adurni had wanted to marry Castanna for a while, then perhaps his behavior when alone with Spinella had been misunderstood.

Trying to seduce a woman's sister does not facilitate romance with that woman.

Lord Auria said again to Castanna, "I ask you to please speak."

Spinella said, "The courtship's somewhat quick, and the match seems agreed on."

The people who had agreed that Lord Adurni should marry Castanna were Lord Auria and Lord Adurni.

Spinella continued, "Do not, sister, reject the use of fate."

Castanna said, "I dare not question the will of Heaven."

Malfato said about the upcoming marriage, "Unthought-of and unlooked-for!"

"My ever-honored lord!" Spinella said to her husband.

Aurelio said, "This marriage frees each circumstance of jealousy."

Aurelio was overstating this. True, if Lord Adurni were to marry Castanna, then since he had a wife at home, a wife who was Spinella's sister, he would be less likely to lust after Spinella. Still, though it is rare, some men commit adultery with their wife's sister.

Lord Auria said, "Make no scruple, Castanna, about the choice of Lord Adurni as a husband. It is firm and real.

"Why else have I so long with tameness nourished report of wrongs, except that I fixed on issue of my desires?"

He had nourished gossip by not taking action such as fighting a duel, but he had not taken action because he wanted better outcomes: Spinella's name cleared, and friendship restored among all the people now present.

A marriage alliance between Lord Auria and Lord Adurni would help maintain peace. They would be brothers-in-law.

Lord Auria continued, "Italians use not dalliance, but execution."

Italians are quick to fight.

He continued, "Herein I degenerated from the custom of our nation."

"Degenerate" is a stronger, more negative word than "deviate."

He had not acted the way many Italians would have acted. Why not?

He continued, "Because the virtues of my Spinella are rooted in my soul. Not rooted in my soul is the common form of matrimonial compliments, which are short-lived, as are their pleasures."

The common form of matrimonial compliments, whatever they are, is superficial. These compliments and their pleasures are short-lived. Possibly, these are the matrimonial compliments that are given between husband and wife when a marriage takes place because the husband has money and the wife has beauty.

Lord Auria said to Spinella, "Yet, truly, my dearest, I might blame your needless absence. My love and nature were no strangers to you.

"But since you were in the house of Malfato, your kinsman, I honor his hospitable friendship, and I must thank it.

"May we now have a lasting truce on all hands."

Aurelio said to Spinella, "You will pardon a rash and over-busy curiosity and nosiness."

He was admitting that he was at fault, and he was asking for her forgiveness.

Spinella said, "That was to blame, but the successful and happy outcome we see here pardons it."

Lord Adurni said to Malfato, "Sir, what presumptions formerly have grounded opinion of unfitting carriage to you, on my part I shall faithfully acquit at easy summons."

He was using legal terminology to say that he hoped Malfato would change his opinion of him, which formerly had been unfavorable. He knew that Malfato loved Spinella and blamed him for what at least seemed to be an attempt to seduce her.

Malfato said, "You act early and so forestall the need for any fancy apologies. Use your own pleasure."

This meant: Do what you want to do.

Malfato had seemed shocked when Lord Auria had given Castanna to be Lord Adurni's wife. Possibly, Malfato had been interested in her. Possibly, Lord Adurni knew that.

Benazzi rushed in with his sword drawn, followed by Levidolce and Martino.

"What's the matter?" Aurelio asked.

"Matter?" Lord Auria asked.

"Lord Adurni and Malfato found together!" Benazzi said. "Now for a glorious vengeance."

"Hold him! Oh, hold him!" Levidolce said.

Apparently, Levidolce's plan had been to have Benazzi kill Lord Adurni and Malfato. If so, she may have changed her mind just as her plan seemed to be playing out. But was this reformation, if it was one, genuine, or was it a "reformation"? And had Martino agreed to assist in a plot to murder Lord Adurni and Malfato? That seems unlikely.

"This is no place for murder," Aurelio said to Benazzi. "Yield thy sword."

"Yield it, or I will force it," Lord Auria said.

Lord Auria disarmed Benazzi and then asked him, "Do you set up your shambles of slaughter in my presence?"

A shambles is a slaughterhouse.

"Let him come at me," Lord Adurni said.

"What can the ruffian mean?" Malfato asked.

"I have been prevented from getting my vengeance," Benazzi said. "If I had not been, then the temple or the chamber of the Duke would not have proved to be a sanctuary.

"Lord Adurni, thou have dishonorably wronged my wife."

"Thy wife!" Lord Adurni said. "I don't know her, and I don't know thee."

He did not recognize Benazzi and so he did not know to whom Benazzi was married.

"Fear nothing," Lord Auria said.

To whom was he speaking? Spinella and Castanna? Levidolce? If Levidolce, he was saying this: Don't be afraid to speak up.

Levidolce said to Lord Adurni, "Yes, you know me. Heaven has a gentle mercy for penitent offenders."

She then said, "Blessed ladies, don't regard me as a cast-off reprobate, although once I fell into some lapses that our sex are often entangled by, yet what I have been concerns me now no more, for I am resolved to lead a new life.

"This gentleman, Benazzi, disguised as you see, I have remarried."

She said to Benazzi, "I knew you at first sight, and now I offer my constant submission to you on account of all my errors."

Martino said to Lord Adurni, "It is true, sir."

Benazzi said, "I take joy in this revelation that Levidolce recognized me, and I am thankful for the change in Levidolce."

Lord Auria said, "Let wonder henceforth cease, for I am partner with Benazzi's counsels, and in them I was the director."

Lord Auria was saying that he had planned with Benazzi some of Benazzi's actions, probably including pretending to want to kill Lord Adurni and Malfato. He may have done that as a test of Levidolce's character: Would she object when the murders seemed about to occur?

Or he was lying because he had recognized Benazzi as a man who had performed good service for him and whom he would like to rescue from severe and perhaps capital punishment?

He continued, "I have seen the man do service in the wars recently past that were worthy of an ample mention — but more about that hereafter; repetitions now of good or bad would constrict time, time for which we have other uses."

Martino said to Benazzi, "Welcome, and welcome forever!"

Levidolce said to Benazzi, "My eyes, sir, shall never receive a look from yours without a blush."

She said to all present, "Please forget all these rash actions; such actions were mine, and only mine."

Much forgiveness was taking place, and Malfato joined in.

"You've found a way to happiness," Malfato said to Lord Adurni. "I honor your conversion."

"Then I am freed," Lord Adurni said to Malfato.

Malfato replied, "You may call me your friend and your servant."

He had forgiven Lord Adurni.

Martino said, "Now all that's mine is theirs."

He welcomed Benazzi as the husband of his great-niece, both of whom would inherit his wealth.

Lord Adurni said, "But let me add an offering to the altar of this peace."

He gave Benazzi and Levidolce money.

Lord Auria asked, "How does Spinella like this? This holiday — special day — of ours deserves to be remembered in the calendar."

Spinella said, "This reformed gentlewoman — Levidolce — must live fair and worthy in my thoughts."

She said to Levidolce, "And indeed you shall."

Castanna said to Levidolce, "And you will live fair and worthy in my thoughts; your reformation requires a friendly love."

Levidolce said to the two sisters, "You're kind and bountiful."

Trelcatio, Futelli, Amoretta, and Piero entered the room, driving in Fulgoso and Guzman.

Trelcatio said, "By your leaves, lords and ladies, I will increase your jollities by bringing mine, too.

"Here's a youngster whom I call my son-in-law, for so my daughter will have it."

He presented Futelli to the group.

Amoretta lisped, "Yeth, in sooth, thee will."

Futelli and she would be married.

Trelcatio said, "Futelli has weaned her from this pair: Fulgoso and Guzman."

Piero said, "Stand forth, resolute lovers."

Futelli and Amoretta stood forth.

Trelcatio said, "They are a top and top-gallant pair — and for his pains she will have him or none. He's not the richest in the parish; but he is a wit: I say 'Amen' because I cannot help it."

Why couldn't he help it? Possibly: 1) he was so happy that he could not help saying it, or 2) he was so unhappy that he could not help saying it.

Chances are, he did not especially want Futelli for a son-in-law, but because he could not prevent the marriage, he accepted it.

Amoretta said, "Tith no matter."

Lord Auria said, "We'll remedy the penury of fortune. Futelli and Amoretta shall go with us to Corsica. Our cousin Amoretta must not despair of means, since it is believed that Futelli can deserve a place of trust."

Is there evidence that Futelli can deserve a place of trust? Futelli had won Amoretta's love, and he had stopped her excessive interest in princes and the number of horses pulling their carriages. Still, he had done this as a result of what seemed like a cruel practical joke.

Futelli said to Lord Auria, "You are in all unfellowed."

He meant, "You are in everything without an equal."

Or, if he had not heard the good news of Lord Auria and Spinella's reconciliation, and if he suspected that Lord Auria was being sarcastic, he meant, "You are in everything without a marriage partner."

Amoretta lisped, "Withely thpoken."

Piero said to Lord Auria, "Think about Piero, sir."

It seemed that Lord Auria was giving Futelli a chance to advance; Piero also wanted a chance to advance.

Lord Auria said, "Piero, yes."

Yes, he would give Piero a job.

He then asked about Fulgoso and Guzman, "But what about these two pretty ones?"

Fulgoso the Parvenu said, "I'll follow the ladies, play at cards, entertain myself, and whistle."

He was not one to follow a military leader.

He continued, "My wealth shall carry me throughout my life: A lazy life is scurvy and debauched."

He was OK with living a lazy, scurvy, and debauched life.

Fulgoso continued, "You go ahead and fight abroad. We'll be gaming at home while you fight. However the dice fall — high or low — here is a brain that can do it."

Do what? Seek entertainment every day.

He then said, "But for my martial brother Don Guzman, please make him a — what do you call it — a setting dog? No, a sentinel. I'll mend his weekly pay by adding to it."

Guzman the Spaniard said, "He shall deserve it."

"He" referred to himself: He was now humbler than when he used the majestic plural, and he was saying that he would do good work and so he would earn the increased salary.

He then said to Lord Auria, "Vouchsafe to me honorable employment."

Fulgoso the Parvenu said to Lord Auria, "By the Virgin Mary, the Don's a generous Don."

Lord Auria said, "It would be unfitting to lose him."

Yes, he would give Guzman a job.

He then said to all present, "The duties of command limit us to enjoy only a short time for revels. We must be thrifty in enjoying the revels and not waste the time allotted for them.

"No one, I trust, is discontent at these delights; they're free and harmless.

"After distress at sea, the dangers over, safety and welcomes taste better ashore."

EPILOGUE

The court's on rising; it is too late
    To wish the lady in her fate
    Of trial now more fortunate.
    A verdict in the jury's breast
    Will be given up anon [soon] at least;
    Till then it is fit we hope the best.
    Else if there can be any stay,
    Next sitting without more delay,
    We will expect a gentle day.

***

NOTE:

One trial has taken place: the trial of Spinella. The outcome was extremely good for Spinella and everyone else involved in the trial.

But another trial is taking place — in the theater. The play has ended, and so the evidence has been given in the form of acting and directing and producing. Now the jury — the audience — must judge whether the play is good or bad. They will render their decision in the form of applause (or in some cases, lack of it). The actor performing the epilogue hopes for "a gentle day" — a successful play.

APPENDIX A: NOTES
— 1.1 —

[Auria says this:]
The steps
Young ladies tread, left to their own discretion,
However wisely printed, are observed,
And construed as the lookers-on presume:
Point out thy ways, then, in such even paths
As thine own jealousies from others' tongues
May not intrude a guilt, though undeserved.
Admit of visits as of physic forced
Not to procure health, but for safe prevention
Against a growing sickness. In thy use
Of time and of discourse be found so thrifty
As no remembrance may impeach thy rest;
Appear not in a fashion that can prompt
The gazer's eye or holla to report
Some widowed neglect of handsome value.
In recreations be both wise and free;
Live still at home, home to thyself; howe'er
Enriched with noble company, remember
A woman's virtue in her lifetime writes
The epitaph all covet on their tombs.
In short, I know thou never wilt forget
Whose wife thou art, nor how upon thy lips
Thy husband at his parting sealed this kiss.
[He kisses her.]
No more.
(1.1.103-126)

Source of Quotation: John Ford, *The Lady's Trial*. Lisa Hopkins, ed. Manchester and New York: Manchester University Press, 2011.

Many passages in *The Lady's Trial* have more than one meaning. Often one meaning is positive and the other negative. One of the themes in *The Lady's Trial* is the use of language to influence others. Sometimes language is used to influence how others interpret events. Ambiguous language may be used to hide the truth or part of the truth, or to bring about a happy ending. Here I simply list some relevant definitions from the *Oxford English Dictionary* for the above passage. Readers are welcome to examine if and sometimes how different definitions change the meanings of the passages.

The steps
Young ladies tread, left to their own discretion,
However wisely printed, are observed,
And construed as the lookers-on presume: (1.1.103-106)

Wise:

"Of action, speech, personal attributes, etc.: Proceeding from, indicating, or suggesting sound judgement or good sense; 'becoming a wise man' (Johnson); sage." (I.1.b.)

"*spec.* Skilled in magic or hidden arts. Now only dialect, as in *wise wife*" (I.2.b.)

Print:

"*figurative.* To direct or focus (one's gaze, sunbeams, etc.) upon something." (I.1.b.)

"To cause (a manuscript, book, etc.) to be printed; to give to the press; to publish." (II.9.a.)

***

Point out thy ways, then, in such even paths
  As thine own jealousies from others' tongues
  May not intrude a guilt, though undeserved. (1.1.107-109)

Point:

"To mark with or as with points, to punctuate." (point, v1, II.)

"To direct, or give direction." (point, v1, III.)

"To set one's mind or aim at; to direct one's course or move for, towards, or to; to be intent upon." (point, v1, III.9.b.)

To Point Out:

"To direct someone's gaze or attention towards (with, or as with, the finger, etc.); to remark on; to distinguish or separate, to draw attention to." (Phrasal verbs, 1.)

"To draw attention to the fact; to explain or show (that something is the case)." (Phrasal verbs, 2.)

Jealousy:

"Zeal or vehemence of feeling against some person or thing; anger, wrath, indignation." (1)

"Zeal or vehemence of feeling in favour of a person or thing; devotion, eagerness, anxiety to serve." (2)

"Solicitude or anxiety for the preservation or well-being of something; vigilance in guarding a possession from loss or damage." (3)

***

Admit of visits as of physic forced
  Not to procure health, but for safe prevention
  Against a growing sickness. (1.1.110-112)

Physic:

"A medicinal substance; spec. a cathartic, a purgative." (I.1.)

Physic finger:

"*rare* (now *archaic*) the fourth, or ring, finger; = medical finger[1]" (Compounds, C2)
Forced:
"To use violence to; to violate, ravish (a woman)." (Force, v1, I.1.)
"To constrain by force (whether physical or moral); to compel; to overcome the resistance of." (Force, v1, I.3.a.)
"To put a strained sense upon (words)." (Force, v1, I.3.b.)

***

In thy use
Of time and of discourse be found so thrifty
As no remembrance may impeach thy rest; (1.1.112-114)
Thrifty:
"Characterized by success or prosperity (see thrift n.1 1[2]); thriving, prosperous, well-to-do, successful, flourishing; fortunate." (1)
"Of a person: Worthy, worshipful, estimable, respectable, well-living." (2a)
"Well-husbanded." (4b)
Impeach:
"To impede, hinder, prevent." (1.a.)
"To bring a charge or accusation against; to accuse *of,* charge *with*." (4)
Rest:
"Sleep, repose; the feeling of having been refreshed or restored through this." (Rest, n.1, I.1.a.)
"Freedom from trouble, distress, molestation, aggression, etc.; a state of peace, security, or tranquillity." (Rest, n.1, I.3.a. — from 1522)
"Perhaps: a socket into which the bolt of a gate is slid." (Rest, n.1, II.8.)
"An act of seizing or taking into custody a person, goods, etc.; seizure, capture." (Rest, n. 2, 4)

***

Appear not in a fashion that can prompt
The gazer's eye or holla to report
Some neglect of handsome value. (1.1.115-117)
Fashion:
"The action or process of making. Hence, the 'making' or workmanship as an element in the value of plate or jewellery." (1)
"*esp.* with reference to attire: a particular 'cut' or style." (3.b.)
Holla:
"An exclamation meaning Stop! cease!" (A.1.)

---

1. https://www-oed-com.proxy.library.ohio.edu/view/Entry/115684#eid37535698

2. https://www-oed-com.proxy.library.ohio.edu/view/Entry/201245#eid18656529

"A shout to excite attention." (A.2.)

Widowed:

"To cause (a woman) to become a widow; to bereave (a woman) of her spouse. Also occasionally: to cause (a man) to become a widower." (Widow, v. 1.a.)

"*figurative.* To deprive of something essential, important, or highly valued; to bereave; to dispossess." (Widow, v. 1.b.)

Handsome:

"Of conduct, etc.: conforming to what is expected or approved; seemly; courteous, gracious. Now in stronger sense: generous, magnanimous; morally admirable." (A.2.a.)

"Of a person (occasionally an animal): attractive and pleasing in appearance, esp. in having a well-proportioned figure and noble bearing; (now) spec. (of a woman) striking, stately, as opposed to conventionally beautiful or pretty; (of a man) good-looking. Also of the face, figure, etc." (A.4.a)

***

In recreations be both wise and free;
  Live still at home, home to thyself; howe'er
  Enriched with noble company, (1.1.118-120)

Recreation:

"The action or fact of refreshing or entertaining oneself through a pleasurable or interesting pastime, amusement, activity, etc. (esp. habitually); amusement, entertainment." (3.a)

Re-creation:

"The action or process of creating again or in a new way; the result of this process, a new creation." (1)

Wise:

"Of action, speech, personal attributes, etc.: Proceeding from, indicating, or suggesting sound judgement or good sense; 'becoming a wise man' (Johnson); sage." (1.b.)

"*spec.* Skilled in magic or hidden arts. Now only dialect, as in *wise wife*" (2.b.)

Free:

"Of character and conduct: noble, honourable, generous, magnanimous." (A adj.I.3.a.)

"Released from ties, obligations, or constraints upon one's action. Often used with reference to love and marriage; sometimes also (chiefly Scottish) with the sense 'unmarried, single'. (A adj.7.a.)

"Guiltless, innocent, acquitted." (A adj.8.)

Noble:

"Of a person or people: illustrious or distinguished by virtue of position, character, or exploits." (noble, adj. I 1.a.)

"Of a person or people: illustrious or distinguished by virtue of rank, title, or birth; belonging to a high social rank, esp. one recognized or conferred by a sovereign or head of state." (noble, adj. I 2.a.)

"Of birth, blood, family, etc. " (noble, adj. I 2.b.)

Company:

"The fact or state of being with another or others, esp. friends or friendly people; the presence of a companion or companions." (2.a.)

"Sexual intercourse." (2.b.)

***

[R]emember
> *A woman's virtue in her lifetime writes*
> *The epitaph all covet on their tombs. (1.1.120-122)*

Punctuated differently, we have:

howe'er
> *Enriched with noble company, remember*
> *A woman's virtue in her lifetime writes*
> *The epitaph all covet on their tombs. (1.1.118-122)*

Noble:

"Of a person or people: illustrious or distinguished by virtue of position, character, or exploits." (noble, adj. I 1.a.)

"Of a person or people: illustrious or distinguished by virtue of rank, title, or birth; belonging to a high social rank, esp. one recognized or conferred by a sovereign or head of state." (noble, adj. I 2.a.)

"Of birth, blood, family, etc. " (noble, adj. I 2.b.)

Company:

"The fact or state of being with another or others, esp. friends or friendly people; the presence of a companion or companions." (2.a.)

"Sexual intercourse." (2.b.)

Covet:

"To desire; esp. to desire eagerly, to wish for, long for." (1)

"To desire with concupiscence or with fleshly appetite." (2.a.)

Tomb:

"A place of burial; an excavation, chamber, vault, or other space used for the interment of the dead; a grave." (1.a.)

"figurative and in figurative contexts. Something likened to a tomb, esp. in being impenetrable, final, or impossible to return from; spec. the notional resting place of something which is extinct, forgotten, or past; a place where something comes to an end." (3)

***

In short, I know thou never wilt forget
> *Whose wife thou art, nor how upon thy lips*
> *Thy husband at his parting sealed this kiss.*
> *[He kisses her.]*

No more. (1.1.123-126)

Seal:

"To place a seal upon (a document) as evidence of genuineness, or as a mark of authoritative ratification or approval." (Seal v1.I.1.a.)

"To conclude, ratify, render binding (an agreement, etc.) by affixing the seals of the parties to the instrument. Also figurative, to ratify or clinch (a bargain) by some ceremonial act." (Seal v1.I.1.c.)

"To impose (an obligation, a penalty) *on* a person in a binding manner." (Seal v1.I.1.e.)

$$— 4.3 —$$

[Lord Adurni says this:]

> *"Could your looks*
> *Borrow more clear serenity and calmness*
> *Than can the peace of a composed soul,*
> *Yet I presume report of my attempt,*
> *Trained by a curiosity in youth,*
> *Forescattering clouds before 'em, hath raised tempests*
> *Which will at last at break out."* (4.3.9-15)

Source of Quotation: John Ford, *The Lady's Trial*. Lisa Hopkins, ed. Manchester and New York: Manchester University Press, 2011.

This is ambiguous.

"Report" can mean 1) gossip or 2) Aurelio's report to Lord Auria.

"Attempt" can mean 1) "attempt at seduction" or 2) "attempt at providing especially good hospitality."

"Trained" can mean 1) "to have set a trap" or 2) "taught."

"Youth" can mean 1) Lord Adurni or 2) Aurelio's youth.

"Curiosity" can mean 1) "desire to know too much" or 2) "careful attention to detail."

"Forescattering" could possibly be "for scattering."

"'em" can mean "more clear serenity and calmness" and "the peace of a composed soul."

Therefore, "... yet I presume that report of my attempt, / trained by a curiosity in youth / forescattering clouds before 'em ..." can mean:

Lord Adurni is Guilty of Attempted Seduction

"... yet I presume that report of my attempt at the seduction of your wife, which was a result of a trap I set because my youth made me want to acquire knowledge of what it would be like to have sex with her although such a desire for knowledge I ought not to have has had the result of gossip-scattering clouds that obscure clear serenity and calmness and the peace of a composed soul ...."

Or:

Aurelio is Guilty of Being Too Suspicious

"... yet I presume that Aurelio's misleading report of my attempt at providing especially good hospitality, a report that was brought about because Aurelio, who was paying too much attention when keeping an eye on your wife and who was overly curious about what was happening between your wife and me behind closed doors, character traits that he apparently learned in youth, had the result of gossip-spreading clouds that obscure clear serenity and calmness and the peace of a composed soul ...."

— 4.3 —

[Lord Adurni says this:]

Yet as I wish belief, or do desire
A memorable mention, so much majesty
Of humbleness and scorn appeared at once
In fair, in chaste, in wise Spinella's eyes
That I grew dull in utterance, and one frown
From her could every flame of sensual appetite —

Auria says this:

On, sir, and do not stop. (4.3.81-87)

Source of Quotation: John Ford, *The Lady's Trial*. Lisa Hopkins, ed. Manchester and New York: Manchester University Press, 2011.

In this book, I used Henry Weber's "cool'd" rather than "could."

If I had used "could," I would have written this:

He continued, "Yet, as I wish belief, or desire an honorable reputation, so much majesty of humbleness and scorn appeared at once in fair, in chaste, in wise Spinella's eyes that I grew dull in utterance, and one frown from her could every flame of sensual appetite —"

Not liking what he was hearing, Lord Auria interrupted, "Go on, sir, and do not stop."

The purpose of the interruption was to give Lord Adurni a moment to think this: Do I really want to finish that sentence?

— 5.2 —

John Conington translated Horace's *Carmina*, Book 3, Poem 14, lines 25-26 in this way:
 Soon palls the taste for noise and fray,
 When hair is white and leaves are sere:
 Source: Horace. *The Odes and Carmen Saeculare of Horace*. John Conington, trans. London: George Bell and Sons, 1882.
 <https://tinyurl.com/y6zz7tz5>.

— Entire Play —

The main weakness of John Ford's play is probably the Levidolce and Benazzi subplot. Presumably Levidolce wants Benazzi to kill Lord Adurni and Malfato. Why then does she yell for Benazzi to be stopped when he has the chance to try to kill them? Also, Lord Auria says that he was in league with Benazzi, but this is not explained any further.

But it may not be the weakness that it appears to be. A major theme of Ford's play is ambiguity. Over and over, sentences appear that can plausibly be interpreted in two very different and sometimes contradictory ways. The ambiguity here can be this: Does Levidolce ever mean it when she wishes to reform, and if so, when? One cause of ambiguity is lack of information, and in her part of the plot we have a lack of information.

Or this could be just bad plotting on Ford's part, or it could be the case that the printed play left out some important passages. Certainly, Martino's role in the plot is never explained. (At the end of 5.1, Levidolce is going to tell him what his role will be.)

I enjoyed the subplot involving Amoretta. That she ends up with Futelli is foreshadowed, but not fully explained because Amoretta had said that she would take the advice of her father in the future, and her father apparently doesn't like Futelli as a son-in-law. Amoretta's ending up with Futelli also shows that she has not become as intelligent as one would hope.

Other than these weaknesses, this play was much better than I expected it to be. Auria and Spinella are both admirable. Aurelio acts from understandable but sometimes misguided motives, as does Lord Adurni. The main plot was interesting and has shades of grey: The main plot elevates this play.

The deliberately ambiguous passages will make this play difficult for the audience to understand when presented on the stage, but more literary criticism will be welcome.

APPENDIX B: ABOUT THE AUTHOR

It was a dark and stormy night. Suddenly a cry rang out, and on a hot summer night in 1954, Josephine, wife of Carl Bruce, gave birth to a boy — me. Unfortunately, this young married couple allowed Reuben Saturday, Josephine's brother, to name their first-born. Reuben, aka "The Joker," decided that Bruce was a nice name, so he decided to name me Bruce Bruce. I have gone by my middle name — David — ever since.

Being named Bruce David Bruce hasn't been all bad. Bank tellers remember me very quickly, so I don't often have to show an ID. It can be fun in charades, also. When I was a counselor as a teenager at Camp Echoing Hills in Warsaw, Ohio, a fellow counselor gave the signs for "sounds like" and "two words," then she pointed to a bruise on her leg twice. Bruise Bruise? Oh yeah, Bruce Bruce is the answer!

Uncle Reuben, by the way, gave me a haircut when I was in kindergarten. He cut my hair short and shaved a small bald spot on the back of my head. My mother wouldn't let me go to school until the bald spot grew out again.

Of all my brothers and sisters (six in all), I am the only transplant to Athens, Ohio. I was born in Newark, Ohio, and have lived all around Southeastern Ohio. However, I moved to Athens to go to Ohio University and have never left.

At Ohio U, I never could make up my mind whether to major in English or Philosophy, so I got a bachelor's degree with a double major in both areas, then I added a Master of Arts degree in English and a Master of Arts degree in Philosophy. Yes, I have my MAMA degree.

Currently, and for a long time to come (I eat fruits and veggies), I am spending my retirement writing books such as *Nadia Comaneci: Perfect 10*, *The Funniest People in Dance*, *Homer's* Iliad: *A Retelling in Prose*, and *William Shakespeare's* Othello: *A Retelling in Prose*.

By the way, my sister Brenda Kennedy writes romances such as *A New Beginning* and *Shattered Dreams*.

APPENDIX C: SOME BOOKS BY DAVID BRUCE

Retellings of a Classic Work of Literature

Arden of Faversham: *A Retelling*

Ben Jonson's The Alchemist: *A Retelling*

Ben Jonson's The Arraignment, or Poetaster: *A Retelling*

Ben Jonson's Bartholomew Fair: *A Retelling*

Ben Jonson's The Case is Altered: *A Retelling*

Ben Jonson's Catiline's Conspiracy: *A Retelling*

Ben Jonson's The Devil is an Ass: *A Retelling*

Ben Jonson's Epicene: *A Retelling*

Ben Jonson's Every Man in His Humor: *A Retelling*

Ben Jonson's Every Man Out of His Humor: *A Retelling*

Ben Jonson's The Fountain of Self-Love, or Cynthia's Revels: *A Retelling*

Ben Jonson's The Magnetic Lady, or Humors Reconciled: *A Retelling*

Ben Jonson's The New Inn, or The Light Heart: *A Retelling*

Ben Jonson's Sejanus' Fall: *A Retelling*

Ben Jonson's The Staple of News: *A Retelling*

Ben Jonson's A Tale of a Tub: *A Retelling*

Ben Jonson's Volpone, or the Fox: *A Retelling*

Christopher Marlowe's Complete Plays: Retellings

Christopher Marlowe's Dido, Queen of Carthage: *A Retelling*

Christopher Marlowe's Doctor Faustus: *Retellings of the 1604 A-Text and of the 1616 B-Text*

Christopher Marlowe's Edward II: *A Retelling*

Christopher Marlowe's The Massacre at Paris: *A Retelling*

Christopher Marlowe's The Rich Jew of Malta: *A Retelling*

Christopher Marlowe's Tamburlaine, Parts 1 and 2: *Retellings*

Dante's Divine Comedy: *A Retelling in Prose*

Dante's Inferno: *A Retelling in Prose*

Dante's Purgatory: *A Retelling in Prose*

Dante's Paradise: *A Retelling in Prose*

The Famous Victories of Henry V: *A Retelling*

From the Iliad *to the* Odyssey: *A Retelling in Prose of Quintus of Smyrna's* Posthomerica

George Chapman, Ben Jonson, and John Marston's Eastward Ho! *A Retelling*

George Peele's The Arraignment of Paris: *A Retelling*

George Peele's The Battle of Alcazar: *A Retelling*

George Peele's David and Bathsheba, and the Tragedy of Absalom: *A Retelling*

George Peele's Edward I: *A Retelling*

George Peele's The Old Wives' Tale: *A Retelling*

George-a-Greene: *A Retelling*
The History of King Leir: *A Retelling*
Homer's Iliad: *A Retelling in Prose*
Homer's Odyssey: *A Retelling in Prose*
J.W. Gent.'s The Valiant Scot: *A Retelling*
Jason and the Argonauts: A Retelling in Prose of Apollonius of Rhodes' Argonautica
John Ford: Eight Plays Translated into Modern English
John Ford's The Broken Heart: *A Retelling*
John Ford's The Fancies, Chaste and Noble: *A Retelling*
John Ford's The Lady's Trial: *A Retelling*
John Ford's The Lover's Melancholy: *A Retelling*
John Ford's Love's Sacrifice: *A Retelling*
John Ford's Perkin Warbeck: *A Retelling*
John Ford's The Queen: *A Retelling*
John Ford's 'Tis Pity She's a Whore: *A Retelling*
John Lyly's Campaspe: *A Retelling*
John Lyly's Endymion, The Man in the Moon: *A Retelling*
John Lyly's Galatea: *A Retelling*
John Lyly's Love's Metamorphosis: *A Retelling*
John Lyly's Midas: *A Retelling*
John Lyly's Mother Bombie: *A Retelling*
John Lyly's Sappho and Phao: *A Retelling*
John Lyly's The Woman in the Moon: *A Retelling*
John Webster's The White Devil: *A Retelling*
King Edward III: *A Retelling*
Mankind: *A Medieval Morality Play* (A Retelling)
Margaret Cavendish's The Unnatural Tragedy: *A Retelling*
The Merry Devil of Edmonton: *A Retelling*
The Summoning of Everyman: *A Medieval Morality Play* (A Retelling)
Robert Greene's Friar Bacon and Friar Bungay: *A Retelling*
The Taming of a Shrew: *A Retelling*
Tarlton's Jests: A Retelling
Thomas Middleton's A Chaste Maid in Cheapside: *A Retelling*
Thomas Middleton's Women Beware Women: *A Retelling*
Thomas Middleton and Thomas Dekker's The Roaring Girl: *A Retelling*
Thomas Middleton and William Rowley's The Changeling: *A Retelling*
The Trojan War and Its Aftermath: Four Ancient Epic Poems
Virgil's Aeneid: *A Retelling in Prose*
William Shakespeare's 5 Late Romances: Retellings in Prose
William Shakespeare's 10 Histories: Retellings in Prose
William Shakespeare's 11 Tragedies: Retellings in Prose
William Shakespeare's 12 Comedies: Retellings in Prose

William Shakespeare's 38 Plays: Retellings in Prose
William Shakespeare's 1 Henry IV, aka Henry IV, Part 1: A Retelling in Prose
William Shakespeare's 2 Henry IV, aka Henry IV, Part 2: A Retelling in Prose
William Shakespeare's 1 Henry VI, aka Henry VI, Part 1: A Retelling in Prose
William Shakespeare's 2 Henry VI, aka Henry VI, Part 2: A Retelling in Prose
William Shakespeare's 3 Henry VI, aka Henry VI, Part 3: A Retelling in Prose
William Shakespeare's All's Well that Ends Well: A Retelling in Prose
William Shakespeare's Antony and Cleopatra: A Retelling in Prose
William Shakespeare's As You Like It: A Retelling in Prose
William Shakespeare's The Comedy of Errors: A Retelling in Prose
William Shakespeare's Coriolanus: A Retelling in Prose
William Shakespeare's Cymbeline: A Retelling in Prose
William Shakespeare's Hamlet: A Retelling in Prose
William Shakespeare's Henry V: A Retelling in Prose
William Shakespeare's Henry VIII: A Retelling in Prose
William Shakespeare's Julius Caesar: A Retelling in Prose
William Shakespeare's King John: A Retelling in Prose
William Shakespeare's King Lear: A Retelling in Prose
William Shakespeare's Love's Labor's Lost: A Retelling in Prose
William Shakespeare's Macbeth: A Retelling in Prose
William Shakespeare's Measure for Measure: A Retelling in Prose
William Shakespeare's The Merchant of Venice: A Retelling in Prose
William Shakespeare's The Merry Wives of Windsor: A Retelling in Prose
William Shakespeare's A Midsummer Night's Dream: A Retelling in Prose
William Shakespeare's Much Ado About Nothing: A Retelling in Prose
William Shakespeare's Othello: A Retelling in Prose
William Shakespeare's Pericles, Prince of Tyre: A Retelling in Prose
William Shakespeare's Richard II: A Retelling in Prose
William Shakespeare's Richard III: A Retelling in Prose
William Shakespeare's Romeo and Juliet: A Retelling in Prose
William Shakespeare's The Taming of the Shrew: A Retelling in Prose
William Shakespeare's The Tempest: A Retelling in Prose
William Shakespeare's Timon of Athens: A Retelling in Prose
William Shakespeare's Titus Andronicus: A Retelling in Prose
William Shakespeare's Troilus and Cressida: A Retelling in Prose
William Shakespeare's Twelfth Night: A Retelling in Prose
William Shakespeare's The Two Gentlemen of Verona: A Retelling in Prose
William Shakespeare's The Two Noble Kinsmen: A Retelling in Prose
William Shakespeare's The Winter's Tale: A Retelling in Prose

www.ingramcontent.com/pod-product-compliance
Lightning Source LLC
Chambersburg PA
CBHW031325160726
47993CB00002B/544